Dear Paul...

am I the only one?

Dear Paul...

am I the only one?

—— Bridget Plass ——

Published by
BRF
First Floor, Elsfield Hall
15–17 Elsfield Way, Oxford OX2 8FG
ISBN 1 84101 038 3

First published 2001
10 9 8 7 6 5 4 3 2 1

Acknowledgments
Unless otherwise stated, scripture quotations are taken from The New
Revised Standard Version of the Bible, Anglicized Edition, copyright © 1989,
1995 by the Division of Christian Education of the National Council of the
Churches of Christ in the USA, and are used by permission. All rights
reserved.

Scripture quotations taken from the Holy Bible, New International Version,
copyright © 1973, 1978, 1984 by International Bible Society, are used by
permission of Hodder & Stoughton Limited. All rights reserved. 'NIV' is a
registered trademark of International Bible Society. UK trademark number
1448790.

Scriptures quoted from the Good News Bible published by The Bible
Societies/HarperCollins Publishers Ltd, UK © American Bible Society 1966,
1971, 1976, 1992, used with permission.

A catalogue record for this book is available from the British Library

Printed and bound in Great Britain by
Omnia Books Limited, Glasgow

Foreword

In her unusual approach to the thrilling, frustrating, and (apparently) never-ending quest to understand Paul and his letters, Bridget Plass follows Paul himself in her creative use of intellect and imagination. She selects for treatment issues that are of abiding relevance, and Paul's supposed reaction to Tricia's pain and perplexity, for example, is the most effective 'bereavement counselling' that I, for one, have ever encountered.

Peggy Knight
Formerly lecturer in theology (at London Bible College) and latterly teacher in Old and New Testament Studies on several lay training schemes.

Introduction

Before you read this book, I want to point out one or two simple facts to those of you who might struggle with the concept of a correspondence taking place between Paul and a group of 21st-century men and women. To start with, this book is fictional. Admittedly all Paul's 'replies' are based as closely as I could manage on facts drawn from Acts and from his letters, but it is indisputably a work of fiction. Of course it is not possible for such a correspondence to take place. Neither does it imply that I believe in contacting the saints. It is quite simply a case of 'What if...?'

What if it were possible to ask Paul all the questions we would like to ask and to challenge him on his more controversial statements. What might he have to say to us? I don't know how he would choose to reply if we wrote to him, but trying to guess has been great fun. I hope my guesses might prove helpful to those of you who have struggled to reconcile some of Paul's most famous declarations with some of his most dogmatic. You may, of course, totally disagree with the replies I credit to Paul: 'He'd never have said that!' If so, try writing your own. Or use the letters from Madge and co. as discussion starting points on how you think Paul would have responded.

Let me share with you a couple of typical reactions I have encountered when telling friends what I am trying to do. The first is from my male friends. Do you know, I hadn't realized that the cerebral understanding of Pauline thought has been considered such a male prerogative until I registered the surprise and, dare I say, kindly doubt in their eyes! The second is from some of my female friends who have expressed their disgust that Paul, whom they consider a priggish, narrow-minded little misogynist, should receive such intense focus from a woman!

So why did I want to try to discover what Paul might have to say to individuals struggling with the pressures of a post-modern world? First, because there is no other figure in the Bible who has produced such a passionate response in me. I passionately love, hate, respect and despise the things he has written.

The second is that I confess I am ashamed at the way that many women of today dismiss what Paul has to say on the role of women within marriage and the Church, without really giving him the benefit of the doubt. I consider us worthy of more than that. Whether we like to admit it or not, we are rather in his debt. God himself chose Paul to bring the good news to us, the Gentiles. The word Ananias uses when he tells Paul that he has been singled out for this immense task is the same verb, *eklegomia*, that is used in Luke's Gospel when Jesus chooses his twelve apostles. Not only that, but Jesus himself appeared to Paul, thus adding further proof that Paul was uniquely qualified to bear witness. After his resurrection, Jesus appeared to all his apostles, making it clear beyond any shadow of doubt that he was alive. On the road to Damascus he added Paul to the Twelve.

Lastly, God filled Paul with the power of the Holy Spirit, anointing his ministry and allowing him to preach repentance and forgiveness. Paul is the most famous anointed evangelist of all time. The churches he planted planted ours. The words that he wrote and spoke laid the foundations of church practice and doctrine from then to now (quite apart from popping up at every wedding and funeral I have ever been to!) And whatever we may think of some of what he said, he lived out his calling through every hardship imaginable, including shipwrecks, beatings, illness, loneliness and imprisonment. Let's face it, he is no lightweight to be tossed out of our spiritual ring!

So I invite you to join me in the company of this controversial man of God. Just how familiar are we with everything Paul wrote? How much do we know about the cultural context in which he operated? This book aims to catch a glimpse, not only of the passion that drove him on, but also of the compassion he had for those little churches that he founded and the individuals who were involved with them. Perhaps we will come to understand a little better why his 'dear friend the doctor' Luke liked and respected him so much, and why Timothy remained close to him throughout his ministry and appeared to love him dearly. We may even stop seeing him as a single-issue fanatic, and indeed start to question whether our obsession with the comparatively few remarks he made about women puts us in danger of becoming fanatically intolerant towards him.

The first contact

Come on, pull yourself together, you can do this. You said you'd phone him and you will. Oh my goodness—it's ringing now. What have I let myself in for?

Good afternoon. This is the reception hall of heaven. I'm afraid there is no one available to take your call at present. If you would like to leave a message after the long harp-tone, we will be glad to consider your request and get back to you as soon as possible.

Err, hello. Umm, I'm not sure who I'm talking to—whoever's in charge, I suppose. This is a bit embarrassing, but my message is for Paul actually. Paul the apostle? The writer of the letters? You know—the Paul who was struck down on the way to... well, of course you know which one I mean. If you're who I think you are, you appeared to him there! I'm so sorry, you see, I keep forgetting that this is heaven and... oh, gosh, my time must be running out already. The thing is, I wanted to ask him something. You see, what I wanted to ask is a bit of a cheek really, but I've got this group of women here and they're all so upset and confused by him—well, not by him exactly but by what he said about... pretty well everything, really. So I was wondering if it would be all right for them to write to him and, if possible, for you to see your way to letting Paul write back. You see, I'm the secretary of a group in our town called CTC (Churches Together for Christ). We meet regularly and most of our members are women. I feel really sad that so many of them don't seem to feel he would be willing or able to help them. They feel that he despised women when he was alive, so he would despise them now. But I don't see how that can have been true then, and I hope it isn't true now. After all, you chose him rather dramatically to rescue the known world, didn't you? And—well, if it wasn't for him I probably wouldn't be here speaking to you at all.

Can you tell him it's not just an angry mob down here who want to write to him. There are a few men too, and some really desperate friends, some not even in a church, who need advice badly. Oh, and Mrs Flowers!

Well, that is it really, so I'll…

Oh! Hello! I didn't expect… Oh, yes! Yes, of course. Right, I'll tell them, then. Yes, I'll make it clear that the offer is for a limited period only. Yes, of course I will. Well, thank you very much. I'll tell them they can start writing straight away. Thank you. Thank you…

Goodness me—what have I started?

The letterwriters

Madge

Dear Paul

Thank you so much for agreeing to read what I have to say and, if appropriate, to respond. I am very grateful to you for being prepared to give up your valuable time.

I'm not quite sure how to go about this. In fact, I must say that in all my twenty-five years as a junior school headmistress I have never been so nervous about putting pen to paper. For the first time I'm rather acutely aware of how some children's parents must have felt, waiting outside my office to complain about another child's behaviour, or planning how to convey their unhappiness with the way a member of my staff had been treating their little darling! It's something to do with the combination of stomach-churning anxiety, anger and hurt, and an awareness that they only have one chance to put over what they so want to say. I just hope you are not planning to do what I have done so often, which is to try to get the whole thing over as quickly as possible, with the least amount of emotional spillage, simply because of being too frantically busy.

The truth is that what I am about to say, I haven't ever really said to anyone, and certainly never expected to be saying to you face to face—well, letter to letter, anyway. I feel so angry, you see. So angry that you have the audacity to trot out cataclysmic statements without realizing how hard it is for others to be like you. How dare you say—hold on a minute, I'm getting this all wrong. Let me tell you a bit about myself first.

My name is Madge Grey. Until eight years ago it was Madge Potter, but the Potter bit upped and went, so I'm back to being Grey. Someone else has become Potter. Someone apparently less busy and less bossy. Mother of one of the little boys I taught—actually, I was his favourite teacher! Well, I was very good at my job. About the only thing I ever was good at, according to Steven, my husband. He always reckoned I'd have had more time for him if he'd been little and smudgy and wiggly and naughty. Perhaps he was right. When I think what they used to say to me—the parents, I mean.

'I could never do what you do. How do you do it?'

'Always so understanding…'

'You were the one for Karen… for David… for our Julie…'

Just not the one for Steven and perhaps not 'always so understanding' for Jeremy either. Oh, I'm sorry, you don't know. Jeremy is my son. He's 34 now. He doesn't live at home, of course. That's another story. As to 'how I did it', well, the only thing that has given me any sense of achievement for the last three years since I retired is the fact that I get up every morning.

Oh, at first the relief was tangible. Every single morning I relished the dismissal of my old companions, Dread and Fear, with an authoritative, 'You can go now', and settled down to two cups of tea from the teasmaid I bought myself as a little retirement present. I even decided that I liked having my own space—that the future was there to be lived, and that this year I would do my hanging baskets beautifully and finish the tapestry cushion that Jeremy gave me for Christmas four years ago. You never know, I would tell myself, Jeremy might even want to come and stay for a while. I would be able to do all the things with him that somehow there had never seemed time for when I was working. Well, when I say all the things—I suppose he might consider half-hour-long bath times with lots of ducks and splashing a trifle unsuitable! Still, you get the picture. For a little while, I looked at the rest of my life as a child looks at tomorrow on Christmas Eve.

It was *after* that—after the first few months of relief and exhaustion. I found I had new charges tugging my skirts for attention. Loneliness and Despair were two of the most persistent.

'What are we going to do today, Miss?'

'How are we going to fill every minute of every long hour of this seemingly endless day, Miss?'

'I've got an idea, Miss. We can do guilt and fear and hopelessness this morning and after break we can put off popping in to see old Mrs James because we can't think how to walk up the drive and knock on her door. Then we can watch lunchtime TV and go to the shop on the corner and buy two sausages and one potato and no one will say, "I don't know how you do it" and smile at us with love and admiration.

And no one will need us to do up their shoelaces or wipe their nose or be firm or stern or anything, really. And when we go to our counsellor at two-thirty in the everlasting afternoon and he asks us to write down what are the good points about us, we can write "teaching" and cry.'

I'm sorry, Paul. I know that none of this is your fault. But when you say something like, 'I count everything as loss because of the surpassing worth of Jesus Christ my Lord. For his sake I have suffered the loss of all things and count them as refuse,' it makes my blood boil.

You chose your way. I know it must have been horribly hard to stay on it, but at least you chose it. I never wanted to be on my own. I haven't given it away, it was torn from me. It wasn't that I no longer had need of Steven. He no longer had need of me. I was the litter to be thrown away. You sound so right, so sure, so downright smug. How can you possibly understand?

And another thing. You talk of how 'In all things God works for good'! Whose good? Where is the good in feeling useless and rejected and guilty and alone? Tell me, Paul. I really want to know. Now! Stand up straight. Don't scuff the carpet. Look me in the eye.

Oh my goodness! Oh, I'm so sorry. How could I be so rude? I'm afraid I forgot myself. How embarrassing. Once a teacher, always a teacher. That's what they say, isn't it? But that's the problem.

Who am I?

I'm not Steven's wife. I'm not Jeremy's mother. I'm not Daniel's or Karen's or Julie's teacher. I don't take assemblies or staff meetings or make up rotas for dinner ladies or talk to governors. I don't have an office with a door, outside which parents sit and wait until I'm ready for them. I have no opportunities to be kind but fair, or stern but loving. I am nothing. Just a silly, silly woman who has lost everything and counts it all as loss. I need help and I can do with not being burdened by your platitudes.

Yours, confused and angry,

Madge Grey

To Madge

Grace, mercy and peace from God the Father and Christ Jesus our Lord.

It is wonderful to be able to write those words in full assurance that they do love you and wish for you to know that!

Can you imagine how strange it is to find that something you wrote nearly two thousand years ago to support Christians in a church in Philippi is actually affecting an intelligent woman in the 21st century in Britain so much that she feels compelled to write back?

Well, perhaps you can. You must meet strangers all the time who still remember something you said to them when they were very small. Indeed, I recently had the privilege of meeting one of your ex-pupils. Sadly for his family, he had to leave your world when he was only twenty-three. Meningitis, I think his records say. Of course, he is completely well now. Apparently his first down-payment towards a pleasant residence here was made after a certain small incident in your school. Do you remember a little skinny lad with tufty blonde hair, called Barry? He describes himself as being an angry, miserable child when you knew him. Apparently his father was having an affair and Barry had found out. He wasn't able to tell anyone, stopped being able to concentrate and kept getting into fights. It was you he told on a rainy playtime after he had pummelled a schoolmate into the book-corner carpet. According to Barry, you had a big box of pink tissues—which I understand are handkerchiefs—and a tin of chocolate biscuits. For what seemed a whole day, you listened while the rain beat against your study window. You helped him understand that it wasn't his fault. You even helped him tell his father what he had overheard. You suggested that if he felt like hitting out again, he should speak to his Father in heaven, his Daddy God. Oh yes, Madge, you were *the* one for Barry. You *were* a good teacher.

Now, there are one or two things I would like to say to you. The first thing is that we all fail. We try to be perfect but we fail. We fail in our relationships, we fail those we are responsible for, we fail ourselves and we fail God. That is why Jesus had to come. That is why he died. Madge, I can identify with you all too well in the circumstances of your particular failure. I, too, was absorbed in what seemed to me an all-important job. I, too, became consumed by the intensity of my commitment and as a result destroyed those close to me. In my case it did not lead to someone walking out and leaving me; it led to murder. Can you imagine how I managed to live with my memories of the stonings and the screams of the children whose parents I had dragged from their homes to kill publicly and without mercy?

Yes, you neglected Jeremy a bit. Yes, it is true, he is angry with you. He blames you for the fact that his father is no longer with you. There are things you have to put right if you can. Your husband did get the discarded remnant of your famous patience and warmth. He did get sick of your irritability and caustic sarcasm. He could have done with a bit of the pink tissue and hair stroking treatment at times.

I've been able to say sorry to my victims, of course. Stephen in particular was, as you can imagine, absolutely delightful about the whole incident. Claims he never even noticed me holding the cloaks of the men who stoned him to death.

I know your Steven has not had the advantage of knowing the Lord in the same way, but you could write to him. Reconciliation is not an option open to you, because he has married again, but healing is. You remember how John said in his letter, 'Perfect love casts out fear'? Well, tell Steven the truth about your responsibility for the failure of your marriage and one horrible lesson could become a free period. You might even tackle your tapestry!

I'm serious, though. When I sent Onesimus back to Philemon, I had no idea how my old friend would react. It was not usual for runaway slaves to be welcomed on their return as a 'dear brother'—which is how I urged Philemon to respond. I just knew it was right. Right for Onesimus to have a chance to ask for forgiveness and become whole and without fear. Right for Philemon to have an opportunity to forgive and look at the reasons why his slave ran away. Right for both of them to acknowledge their equal status before God as brothers in Christ and forgiven sinners.

At the moment, you have lost all the power you had as a headmistress and, because of your guilt and pride and fear, you are in danger of losing all power over yourself. Through your efforts to sort out your problems yourself, you have put yourself under the law. You have become poverty-stricken because you don't accept your faults as your own possessions, possessions which you have the freedom to give away. In other words, by refusing to accept the grace of forgiveness held out to you by your Lord and Saviour, you have made yourself a slave to the evil one. Onesimus may have been a slave according to the law of the time but in his acceptance of grace he was free in the most real sense, whether his earthly master accepted him as a brother or a slave.

Madge, I am sorry you see the things I wrote as cold and demanding and simplistic. Usually I am accused of being too complicated! But I do perceive what you mean. Words are capable of tidying up experience sometimes to a point where the ragged reality of life gets left out. All I can say is that when I left Damascus, resolved to live out my life as a disciple of the very Messiah I had condemned, some very important things happened to me. I may have lost power over the destiny of others but I also realized that I had lost the manacles of those things which had once owned me.

It is not easy to convey what I felt at that time. Returning to Jerusalem, I was an outcast from every camp. It may look very tidy in Luke's account but, believe me, that was one of those ragged times. I had betrayed the Sanhedrin and everything my Jewish education had taught me up to that point, namely that the proof of the Messiahship would be found in the restoration of Israel from the yoke of Roman colonialism. I had to seek reconciliation with those whom, until then, I had been putting to death by the bucketful. Easily as difficult as getting to Mrs James' front door, don't you think?

Or perhaps not! Anyway, I probably wouldn't have managed to conquer my feelings of guilt and fear at this time if it hadn't been for two things. One was my knowledge that I had gained a new Father who loved me unconditionally whatever I did, had done or would do in the future—the Daddy God you introduced our friend Barry to. This gave me the confidence to truly own what I had done, so that I could freely give it to my newly discovered Father.

The second thing was that I had just acquired a new friend who was determined to help me do what, in my heart, I now knew I must— Barnabas. I wasn't very good at friendship, but he was. It was he who told Peter and the others what had happened to me on the road to

Damascus. It was his belief that I had something I could contribute that got me through their doors.

Madge, listen to me carefully. The things that you have lost are the very things that could be tools for your future career as one of God's full-time workers. They were taken from you without your giving them away. That is true, but now you can throw them away in a different sense. You can take power over your guilt and your fear, acknowledge their part in you, recognize them as litter only fit to be discarded and give them to God. Dear Madge, the very failures that are causing you to despair, and that result in you lashing out at me in much the same way young Barry lashed out at his little friend in the book-corner, can become loaves and fishes that, when broken in the hands of Jesus, will feed the multitudes.

That brings me to what I said to the Christian church in Rome, 'In all things God works for good.'

I didn't mean that everything would be good in the sense of *comfortable* if we accepted Jesus. How could I write that to the church in Rome, where there was a fair chance that they would be thrown to Nero's lions for acknowledging their faith? No, I meant that everything we experience can be used by God to help us to become more like Christ, so that eventually we will be able to live at peace with ourselves.

One last thing, Madge. I know you no longer have a husband, but have you a close friend who will help you to make your peace with your family and start again in a new life—someone you can be completely honest with? The Holy Spirit is very good at working through our friends if they love us and love him. If you haven't got such a friend, you could ask God for that. After all, he supplied Ananias and Barnabas for me at a time when I needed them most but deserved them least, and he provided you for young Barry, so there is a good precedent.

May the grace of the Lord Jesus Christ be with your spirit, Madge, and may you come to understand how deep and wide the love of the Father is for you. Oh, and by the way, just to give you one more thing to think about. Did you know that until I gave Onesimus his name, he did not have the status of a title at all? And did you know Onesimus means 'profitable' or 'useful'? I gave him the name before he went back to face his former master, as a symbol of all he had come to mean to me while I was in prison. You say you don't know who you are, and I know that the way in which you were forced to change your name has caused you great pain and resulted in a real loss of identity. I tell you, it really doesn't matter whether you are Potter or Grey because your name is written in the Book of Life. You are God's child. What name would you like your Father in heaven to give you?

Your brother in Christ,

Paul (formerly known as Saul!)

∽ *Beverley* ∾

Dear Paul

I am really at a loss to understand what all this hoo-ha is about being able to write to you, and I feel I want to challenge your audacity in presuming you have anything to say to the world I inhabit.

My father attended our local Anglican church and always claimed that his faith gave meaning to his life. I have no problem with that if it made him happy. I loved him very much and was quite content to go along with him to his church on high days and holidays. He and I even had infrequent but extremely lively and rather enjoyable discussions on the subject of Christianity before he died. I consider myself fortunate to have had a father who appreciated my independence and freedom of thought. He never pressurized me into believing or made me feel in any way guilty. I can still see his gentle smile and arms-up surrender when I beat him in argument. He used to take his revenge during the game of draughts with which we would often conclude our evenings together. I miss it all, but I have to say that I never heard anything to make me see the relevance of either Jesus Christ or indeed your good self to my life.

Look at it from my point of view. I am 23 years old, female and unmarried. I have a degree in Communications, I work as a PA in a small but successful modelling agency, I already earn a far better salary than my father ever did, I have my own car, my own flat and above all my independence. I awake in the morning to my radio alarm, use my remote control to turn on my television, and listen to an up-to-date news report of exactly what is happening throughout the world. I check my mailbag on my computer and my fax machine for messages. On the basis of these I make phone calls on my mobile phone, arrange my boss's day (incidentally, a woman aged 30), might well have a phone conference, and also pay any urgent bills using my credit card. And that is just in the first half-an-hour of my day!

Be honest, Paul, what do you see when you look at our world? Are you not amazed at our progress, our scientific advances, our sophist-ication? Do you not marvel at what men and women have achieved in the last two hundred years, since religion has ceased to be used by so many as a prop and an easy answer to all mysteries? This is possible because we have decided to take control of our environment. Do you ever wonder what you might have done or said had you been born two thousand years later? Would you still be offering the same advice? Selling the same line? My father trusted you, Sir, so please don't let him down by replying untruthfully.

I await your reply with considerable interest.

Yours sincerely,

B.R. Palmer

Dear B.R. Palmer

Your letter interests me greatly. Reading between the lines, I suspect your delightful father lacked a certain amount of ambition, unlike yourself. You obviously loved him a great deal and miss his company. You also miss his admiration and concern and, dare I suggest, the 'lively discussions' you had about his religion. I believe I have been called the father of modern Christianity and have even been a father figure to one or two of my young evangelists, but the role of surro-gate father you are unconsciously offering me is a new one.

Point number one—I was not unambitious. Indeed, as a young student studying under one of the leading rabbinic teachers of the known world, I was tipped for the top, groomed for a place on the governing body called the Sanhedrin. Neither, my dear young lady friend, was I to be found dressed in an AD50 equivalent of a fawn-coloured knitted cardigan. Do you know anything at all about Tarsus, the place where I grew up? We may not have invented the microchip but we were a pretty sophisticated bunch. Apart from having a university for Stoic studies, Tarsus was considered to be the centre of Greek culture, with a flourishing theatre and sports stadium.

But then, I wouldn't dream of insulting your obvious intelligence by reminding you of the extraordinarily sophisticated lifestyle of both the Greeks and the Romans. I expect you are quite warm in the morning while you make all those important phone calls. Did you enjoy a pleasant hot shower after all that strenuous phoning? Central heating? Any idea who invented it? Oh yes, of course...

So, having got some of the rather slim insults out of the way, let's look more closely at the rest of your letter. What else do our world and yours have in common? You mention the fact that you hear news from all over the world, just as it happens. But does it really happen exactly as you hear it? I believe you have a somewhat dubious newspaper entitled the *News of the World*. Does that say it all? Is it not still the case that political gain, economic interest and individual bias still play a part in determining how much truth you actually receive? Is it not the case that undercover bribery is as prevalent in your world as it was in ours, when Caiphas and the Sanhedrin, motivated purely by self-interest, set out to murder Jesus Christ?

You say you have a degree in Communications. Presumably, then, you have studied the effect of the subtle propaganda machinery employed to a greater or lesser extent by every government in the world since civilization began, sometimes to truly devilish ends.

Are there really no Herods in the 21st century? No leaders prepared to sacrifice the lives of innocents to further the safety, wealth and stature of their personal dynasty? Surely, Ms Palmer, you are not so naïve and unsophisticated as to believe that human nature has progressed? Has illness been eradicated, poverty erased, prejudice purified? Has education for all brought equality? Has liberation brought peace? Is there no loneliness or fear? No evil? No hypocrisy? No brutality?

I cannot comment on your world. I can only instruct from mine, but I am confident that whatever may have changed in the world, the human heart with its capacity to deceive and to be deceived, to corrupt and to be corrupted, has not changed. Neither, I am quite sure, have the eternal hopes and yearnings for personal peace. In AD57, approximately one thousand nine hundred and seventy-eight years before you were born, I was closely involved with the newly planted church in Rome. Even you will have difficulty equating your image of dressing-gowned dodderers with anything you have ever heard of life in Rome! As a society they knew everything there was to know about refinement and decadence but also about excellence. They would have understood ambition! Incidentally, did you know it was possible even for a slave to reach a position of influence in the city?

So what was I doing? What was I offering them? You talk about the prop of religion. You say it was used as a simplistic solution to the mysteries of the universe, and, of course, there is truth in that. There has always been a desire to understand the world. The Romans I was writing to had, as you know, many gods to whom they prayed.

Presumably, you think I was a sort of door-to-door salesman, offering what I had been convinced was a more up-to-date product— a belief system which may have seemed radical at the time, and able to answer questions more thoroughly, but which, in the 21st century, is clearly redundant and rather charmingly old-fashioned. Obviously, you will be expecting me to defend what I did, especially as my way of life involved such high personal risk.

Certainly I do want to say that the job given to me was extremely difficult and nothing like as cosy as you have suggested. It took every bit of my ingenuity and a few out-and-out miracles to get me safely into as many influential situations as possible, but when I got there my message was always the same. Again and again I tried to point out that it is in the glorious mystery of the created world that God's glory, his eternal power and divine nature can be seen—and that when people stop glorifying God the Creator and, in their foolishness, start to worship created things, society becomes so decadent that even children are not safe. You may not have exchanged the glory of an immortal God for images made to look like men and reptiles and animals and birds, but you do seem to have created your own gods, called Computer, Car and even, laughingly, Household Appliance. To me, Jesus was not a take-or-leave alternative to Apollo or Zeus. Nor is he now an alternative to a no-bag vacuum cleaner! I was not offering a free sample of the Holy Spirit with every contract signed. To me it was a matter of life and death whether those who heard my story believed it or not. Jesus was and is the Son of the living God. Only through accepting this by an act of faith and obedience can one become whole and healed and truly alive.

Much as I admire your delightful parent, I cannot condone his *laissez-faire* attitude to your energetically determined lack of belief. Neither do I see your enjoyable arguments about religion as an alternative intelligence test to a game of draughts. It is true that I thought the world as we know it was intended by God to come to an end during my lifetime, and this fuelled my determination to stress the urgency of the need to accept Jesus as the only possible salvation. Such a level of passion didn't leave much room for lightheartedness. Also, I can see why you find the things I stand for such an anachronism. After all, your society is still recovering from a rather disgusting preoccupation with hell that you inherited from the century before. Glancing over the last two thousand years, I have to tell you that I expect to see a massive swing back to religion and faith. That is, if your society has sorted out a more effective way of dealing with spiralling decadence than either Greece or Rome managed! Or unless God decides enough is enough!

Ms Palmer, I refuse to smile at you or to raise my hands in defeat, or to play draughts. The continuation of our discussion is too urgently important to me and, I might add, to your father. Will you pick up the gauntlet I have thrown down? I have all the time in eternity to fight you for your life. It's up to you.

Yours,

Paul

Dear Paul

What do you mean, 'and, I might add, to your father?' Is he with you? Can I talk to him? Can you tell him how much I love him and miss him and wish I'd valued more what he stood for? Can you tell him how lonely I am and how I can't find any meaning in my life? Can you? I'll believe it all if you can prove to me he is with you and I'll do anything to see him again. Anything.

Yours,

Beverley

Dear Beverley

My dear child, how can it be that someone who was clearly greatly loved by her earthly father can place so little value on getting to know her heavenly one?

I can assure you that I am not undervaluing your desire to know more about your father or to receive news from him, but that is not and was never my job. It is only through digging your hands deeply into the wonderful, rich soil that is your heavenly Father's love that you will, by faith, be able to receive the assurances you need. He alone can help you. He wants to. Can you believe he loves you even more than your own father did? Access to his love does not come about through your purchase of an online package from a computer superstore, or a free CD stuck on the front of your favourite magazine. Without your earning it, Christ has bought you access to his Father's heart. Now, here is the uncomfortable bit for a self-sufficient young lady like yourself. He has bought it at enormous cost—his life.

Hoping to hear from you.

Yours,

Paul

Dear Paul

Being constantly busy myself, I am anxious not to take up too much of your time. Thank you for your interesting reply.

Yours,

Beverley

Dear Beverley

Did you really say you were good at draughts? That was a pathetic move to block me. I am happy to concede, but are you sure you want this particular victory?

Your move,

Paul

Dear Paul

The truth is, I'm tired of playing this particular game. It isn't as much fun as when Father was here. Also, I feel very confused and fed up, and I do feel embarrassed at taking up all this time wittering on. You must be getting very bored.

Yours,

Bev

Dear Beverley

Let me reassure you. I have all the time in eternity to argue God's case! Even when I didn't have, I would let it take a very long time indeed.

Beverley, did you know that when I first went to Ephesus, I used three years of my life just to let people air their views at me, and to try my best to argue persuasively, from experience and scripture? I had to, really, because they so loved rhetoric and argument. I knew they wouldn't just accept what I said. They certainly wouldn't have accepted it if I had tried to bully them. It had to become theirs to own.

The first three months were spent in the synagogue, but opposition was so heavy that I decided to move out into neutral territory. I hired a lecture hall in the city. It belonged to a teacher called, would you believe it, Tyrannus. You can guess how strict he was! He used to teach during the morning until about eleven o'clock while I made my living from making tents. Then he'd go home, along with the majority of sane Ephesian citizens, to sleep during the hottest part of the day while I took over.

It was much the same in Corinth. A fellow called Titus Justus lent me his house there. It was very good of him because, as I recall, I used it almost every day for about eighteen months! I had about five hours a day to fight my corner before work restarted in the city. I did love the cut and thrust of a good argument and would very much enjoy parrying with you. The only thing is, Beverley, I suspect you already know in your heart what you want. And I don't just mean your desire to know you are going to see your father again. I can't just pop down to your world to do the honours, but there is a vicar at your father's old church who just might be able to help. If I don't hear from you again I'll know I can start preparing a little celebration for when we finally meet, but please write again if you need to. Even if it takes more than three years!

If not, then I wish you very happy surfing. I can assure you, you are going to find that the love of God is much deeper and wider and more exciting than anything the Internet can offer!

Yours,

Paul

~ *Pauline* ~

Dear Sir

I am a seventeen-year-old A' level student. One of my three subjects is RE and I am president of my school's CU. I attend our local fellowship, believe in the infallibility of the Bible and am a member of Meteors, our church youth group. We lead worship regularly at our church and sometimes go out reaping the harvest in the shopping mall at our nearest big town. We go to all the concerts that come near us and I have been slain in the Spirit once at one of these. I admire what you did very much and after I have left school I want to be an itinerant missionary just like you. It must be so wonderful to be doing the Lord's work and spreading the gospel as you did, praying and getting answers, hearing where you are supposed to go and just going.

I'm not really sure why I'm writing to you except to ask how I can be like you.

Your little sister in Christ,

Pauline Evans (Miss)

P.S. My mother and father want me to go to uni first to do a theology degree, but I think that's a waste of time, don't you?

Dear Pauline

I was so pleased to receive your letter and to hear of your commitment to the Lord Jesus Christ and to spreading the word. Your energy and excitement almost make me want to be back on earth for a while. I would love to hear more of your plans and your dreams. Perhaps my happiest times were the short interludes I had in fellowship with my brothers and sisters in Christ.

You ask for advice on how to be more like me. Oh, Pauline, I don't think you would really have liked to be like me. The loneliness and my own personality were not always much fun. The only advice I would give you with sincerity is to be really honest with God and to allow *him* to advise you at every point. You say it must have been fun always hearing from God and rushing off to do his will. Actually, I only heard directly from him a few times, one of the times recorded by Luke being, I think, when we were on our way to Mysia and I realized I'd got it wrong and that God wanted me to go to Macedonia instead. Usually I followed any leads I got and used my wits and common sense, together with all the other human attributes God had given me to get on with the job.

I think what you might be referring to is something I wrote to my little church in Philippi. Just as a matter of interest, this was the very first church I ever established in Europe and it was actually in Macedonia, which I've just mentioned, so you can see why it was very special to me. Even more interesting is that the letter you have in your Bible was written while I was a prisoner in Rome, so you've got plenty to think about already! I loved this church—they were always very supportive and generous, even if one or two of the ladies did, as I recall, come to verbal blows occasionally!

I've checked it out, and what I wrote to them was, 'Do not worry about anything, but in everything by prayer and supplication with thanksgiving let your requests be made known to God. And the peace of God, which surpasses all understanding, will guard your hearts and minds in Christ Jesus' (Philippians 4:6–7).

Now, Pauline, can you see anything there about snapping our fingers at God and getting what we want, let alone getting it straight away? What I do see, what I saw then, was that worry and panic can cause us feeble humans to turn away from the one person who has the power, and wants to help us. To pray may sometimes feel too simplistic a response to the difficulties we face, but by pouring our hearts out to God (*proseuche* is the Greek word I originally used for that) we are at least allowing the possibility of divine intervention. The only thing is, it may not be exactly as we planned it!

Do you know where almost all the great missionaries who converted your country came from? Well, the clue lies in who invaded your country and established themselves there in AD45. The inventors of straight roads? Yes, of course I mean the Romans.

Have you ever heard the legend about how England got its name? Another clue! *Angleterre* is the way the French refer to your country, I believe. I mean, of course, the story of how two little boys were taken back to Rome as slaves, and with their blond hair and blue eyes caused quite a stir, leading the emperor to refer to them as angels! It took about six hundred years, but it was Augustine, a Christian monk from Rome who began the work of converting you all those years ago. Incidentally he didn't want to be part of the adventure of bringing the good news at all. Apparently, when he got to France he heard such awful rumours about how savage your ancestors were that he scuttled back to Rome and begged Pope Gregory for permission not to go! Thank God and Pope Gregory that he was forced to come. Oh yes, and because it was God's will and God's timing, God had prepared the way by making sure that the wife of Ethelbert, Saxon king of Kent (Augustine's landing place), was already a Christian! Did you know all those facts about your first archbishop of Canterbury? He had to change his plans because God had other plans. Read on!

So, back to Rome. And no, before you ask, it wasn't me who led this extraordinary multi-god-worshipping city to a belief in one almighty God. The Holy Spirit, with the dedicated help of believers, some of whose names never became well known, managed perfectly well without yours truly! But I have to confess, I so wanted to be part of it for all sorts of reasons. Yes, I wanted to be part of the excitement, the challenge and the adventure, but there was another reason. I was desperately anxious to put a stop to some of the sillier teaching about what was considered necessary for the salvation of such very gentile Gentiles before it got started. It seemed to make so much sense for me to be there. I begged God to let me go, and I have to confess I was sure his answer would be yes. Looking back, I cannot believe the confidence with which I wrote from Corinth to the church in Rome announcing my imminent arrival. I had planned to pop in for a short holiday on my way to converting Spain! I just had one administrative task to complete—the transporting of a money gift from the churches in Corinth to the church in Jerusalem. Nothing to it! How wrong was I about God's plans for me and the world at that point! Oh, I got to

Rome all right, two years later, and in chains! In the meantime I was involved in a riot in Jerusalem, detained in Caesarea, shipwrecked on the way to Rome and stranded in Malta for a whole winter!

So was I wrong to so want to be part of the team telling the good news in Rome? Or wrong in begging God to be allowed to go? I honestly don't think so, but I did get the timing very wrong. My way would have meant a pleasant time of fellowship for me and a small group of believers. God's way meant that the gospel was presented to the Sanhedrin in Jerusalem, two Roman governors in Caesarea and, last but not least, the emperor Nero himself.

So, Pauline, hang on to your dreams. Pour out your heart to God. Make your plans. Use your initiative, your imagination and your wits. Be stubborn, be brave and go all out for what you want. Just be a little more prepared than I was for diversions and hold-ups on the way!

Just one more thing. As you no doubt know, I was a theological student. I got the equivalent of a university degree. There were many times in my ministry when I needed every bit of my knowledge of the scriptures to back the new revelations of the Holy Spirit. The intellect and the heart aren't mutually exclusive, you know. I'm not trying to influence you. Nor am I siding with your parents against you. Just give it some thought.

May God always be with you wherever you go and whatever you do.

Your big brother in Christ,

Paul

Mrs R. Flowers

Dear Paul

I am delighted to have the opportunity to thank you for the excellent job you did in promoting the gospel. I particularly want to thank you for laying down the foundations of reasonable behaviour expected from all those who desire admittance to the Christian Church. I personally have no problem whatsoever with your teaching on decorum and decency. I despair, as I am quite sure you do, at the flippancy of attitude shown by many of our younger and, dare I say, more flamboyant members. I have always worn a hat and gloves to church as a sign of respect. My dear husband always says, 'Betty, live and let live,' and doesn't understand why I get so angry, but I've always maintained that tidiness is next to godliness, and I am confident that you will agree with me. After all, we are entering the presence of God, and I hardly think jeans and T-shirts are reasonable attire for such an occasion. You and I come from a generation where respect for elders and betters was properly taught. What is our world coming to?

Another thing, the young members of our church are never satisfied. They spend most of their time complaining, especially the girls. Whatever happened to 'women may be seen but certainly not heard' in church? I know that those were not your exact words, but that is what you meant, isn't it?

What I am writing to ask is if you might consider writing a general letter for our congregation, setting out in language our young people might apply their brains to, the rules which have served our churches so well over the centuries, but which appear to have been totally and arrogantly dismissed by today's youth.

I enclose a SAE and stationery.

Yours sincerely,

Mrs R. Flowers

To whom it may concern

I have been asked to lay down clearly before you the rules which form the foundation of our Christian faith.

There are two:

1. Love the Lord your God with all your heart and with all your strength and with all your might.
2. Love your neighbour as yourself.

There are no commandments greater than these.

All other rules are conditional, depending on the age and traditions of the society you inhabit.

I would ask you as a congregation, young and old, to consider prayerfully what this might mean for each and every one of you.

May the blessing of our Lord Jesus Christ, the love of God and the fellowship of the Holy Spirit be with you.

Paul

Dear Mrs Flowers

Thank you for writing to me to share the problem you perceive in your church. This type of communication is not unfamiliar to me as on many occasions I found myself in the role of long-distance pastor. I can see that there are several things worrying you and, I confess, several things worry me about what you write.

Let me make one thing clear right at the start. You seem to suggest that I was involved in setting down a system of behaviour for all followers of the Way to strictly adhere to. This is not the case. The situation varied from place to place and I prayerfully considered every individual case, passing on to my churches what I received from God in response to my prayers. There were churches, such as the one established in Corinth, which needed some stern advice about control.

But there were others where the priority was promotion of loving tolerance among members. You might well feel that your church comes into the first category. I tentatively suggest that it might well come under the second and, rather than dwelling on what I wrote to the Corinthians about the way they dressed and did their hair, I think you should address what I had to say to the European churches in my general letter, which I understand has come to be known as Ephesians.

I urged them to be patient with each other, to concentrate on building each other up, and above all to make allowances for each other's faults. After all, as I tried to point out to them, we are all in the Spirit together. We may not look the same or sound the same, but we have all been called to the same glorious future, and we have only been given this hope because of the glorious and extraordinary kindness of God, who is over us all and in us all, living through every part of us. That has always been difficult for followers of the Way. We all have a tendency to judge by external appearances, but that is not what God does. Each one of us has a race to run—our own special course. Each one of us is handicapped by aspects of our personality or understanding which cripple us to a lesser or greater extent.

Mrs Flowers, you have been given special gifts by the Holy Spirit, not only to help you run your race to the best of your ability, but also to assist your church to do the same. At present I am unable to discern your gifts because they are hidden under the filthy garb of your hypercritical exterior. However, I do not despair because I know from personal experience that sin can be wiped away by the touch of the Holy Spirit. First, though, you must acknowledge that what you perceive as a strength is, in fact, a weakness—that it is, in fact, your critical nature and arrogant assumptions that are the thorns in your flesh, slowing you down and causing you much pain and aggravation, nothing whatsoever to do with the way the young are behaving and dressing for running their race.

Can I just say to you, dear lady, that I suspect you haven't ever been able to open yourself up to receive your Saviour's love. When you do, you will be so overwhelmed by the depth of his feeling for you that you will be able to acknowledge your weakness, joyfully acknowledging your dependence on his strength and thereby revealing to the world not your virtues but his glory and power.

As a child I had the privilege of watching some of the finest athletes in the world competing in many styles of race. I rather suspect you would have had difficulty in joining me, as the custom for Greek young men was to run naked in my home town of Tarsus! What I observed then was how passion fuelled them, and how they would set their eyes on the finishing line and, forsaking all distractions, forge ahead. This we must also do, but before I leave you I want to bring before your eyes another illustration from the world you inhabit. I have observed the love of running in your young, and in particular some fun races never heard of in my day. I believe one of them is called a three-legged race, where contenders run in twos, joined together at the ankles to give the appearance of having three legs between them. It occurs to me that, in this case, progress is impeded by the couple's inability to run in unison, and that power comes from their being in tune with each other. The illustration from my day helps our understanding of the need to concentrate on individual progress towards the finishing tape which divides life on earth from life with our Father. The illustration from yours serves perhaps to illustrate the need for members of the church to rely on each other's gifts in order to make swift progress together.

Mrs Flowers—please allow me to call you Betty—I want to leave you with the same final greetings I bestowed on my church in Corinth. Aim for perfection, listen to my appeal, be of one mind, live in peace. And the God of love and peace will be with you.

Yours,

Paul

Jill

Dear Paul

I wonder if I am the only person sitting down to write to you with a pile of washing-up sitting threateningly on the side of the sink, a heap of equally disgusting ironing stuffed into the laundry basket, and a dog performing her 'You don't love me enough to walk me' nose-on-paws mime by the kitchen door. Before my three children were eventually bundled off to school, I managed one row over the level of mould in my teenage daughter's room, one spat of fury over the loss of a PE shirt, and one total dissolve into tears over the fact that we had run out of milk! Do you pick up a sense of personal failure here? Actually, I adore my family and I have reason to believe that, despite my faults, they love me. It's just that none of us seems to be terribly functional, and what worries me is that it inevitably carries over into our church life.

One of the things I suppose I want to ask you is, how the heck did you manage to accomplish so much in your life? I mean, you practically converted the world one way and another, didn't you? I have difficulty remembering to feed the budgie. How did you manage to project an image of being in such control? How did you know what to say? I never do.

I had a friend come round the other morning. She lives down the road from me and her nephew has just been diagnosed with leukaemia. She actually came to me because she thought I, being a Christian, would be able to help. We sat in the middle of my usual chaos and I made her a cup of coffee (no biscuits because, guess what…) But the really awful thing was that I couldn't remember a single useful Bible verse. I couldn't seem to give her any answers, and all I kept thinking was, well, the old 'WWJD' thing. Our kids were told about it at Sunday school. They made badges with it on, I seem to remember. You know—'What Would Jesus Do?' But I didn't know. I didn't have a clue what Jesus would have done. The only thing I could be sure of was that he'd have done something. Not like me—giving her a toilet roll to cry into. Oh, how I longed for a beautiful, breezily clean drawing-room with the scent of jasmine wafting through the open French window, a bowl of roses and a nice box of flowery tissues on the shiny coffee table, and, at very least, the comfort of some chocolate digestives!

But it's always like that with me. I never feel I give God much of a reference. For a while, one of my lads played football on Sunday mornings, and I used to go down after church. If we missed coffee, ignored the glares from our daughter and other son who liked the bit after the service best and didn't see the point of going to church at all if they couldn't see their friends afterwards, and hurtled out of church the minute the vicar had blessed us, we could just about make the last ten minutes. But the looks we got as I hobbled across the mud in my best shoes, accompanied by two surly children and a dejected husband! Invariably we had missed our lad's glory moment, or an injury, or even a sending off. The unspoken 'If you really loved him…' hung in the air, and I was made very aware what the general opinion was of parents who put church before their son's interests.

Then there is the whole business of being a good neighbour. I actually think that living in close proximity to us is used by the devil as a form of anti-evangelism. Why my boys, who are actually very skilled on the pitch, are totally incapable of keeping the football within the confines of our garden, or why they seem to feel it incumbent upon them to do a full victory circuit of the garden every time one of them manages to manoeuvre the ball between our two battered apple trees, escapes me, but it doesn't escape our neighbours. They apparently had children who never, ever, ever behaved so appallingly! Somehow I've never quite felt up to asking them along to our 'invite a neighbour' lunches at church. I wonder why!

It isn't just outside our church that we seem to fail, either. We must be the only parents in the history of the church who have had to leave our housegroup because we've had a phone call from our daughter that our boys are slugging it out over the television controller.

The thing is, Paul, I do actually want to get it right. I do want my children to grow up with a desire to follow Christ. I do want to be of use to my community. I even pray for opportunities to share the good news. You will be relieved to hear that I have never felt called into ministry, so I'm not challenging you on that one. The only time I was asked to do a ladies' breakfast talk, the dog was sick just before I left the house and I didn't have time to dry my hair. I toyed with the idea of lying through my teeth and casually referring to the daily morning swim I managed before breakfast, but I couldn't go through with it and stood there looking as though I had come from a far-off land which sported a different climate from the one enjoyed by the rest of the breakfast eaters!

I was brought up to be satisfied with nothing less than an 'A' for my school work. As I don't actually remember ever getting an 'A' for any exam I ever took, it's perhaps small wonder I feel a bit useless!

So, my question to you is, what can I do to change? What can I do to be a more effective witness? I don't expect you to provide me with an instant cure, or an opportunity to address the masses as Paul did on Mars Hill, nor do I want to be a sort of *Stars in Their Eyes* clone. But you must have some tips from your experience about how to pass on the gospel more efficiently than I ever manage.

When I got married, we had my favourite bit of your writing in our service—the bit about love being more important than speaking in tongues and having a great spiritual ministry. I still love it and it brings tears to my eyes when I hear it read aloud, partly because it's so beautifully written but also because I feel now that I'll always fall short of even that. Loving in the way you describe it seems impossibly difficult. 'Love is patient and kind: it is not jealous or conceited or proud.' Well, I don't think I'm proud or conceited or even jealous, but I am hardly ever patient, and I'm often unkind. So many things get on my nerves. My daughter's preoccupation with her hair and her nails, with all the mess that accompanies it, can throw me into a ludicrous fury. My two sons drive me mad in different ways. Because they cannot see the point of ever sitting down to eat together, they never manage to get to the table in time for any meal. They leave their foul sports kits in their bags, obviously thinking some magical meta-morphosis can take place whereby their smelly, mud-laden shorts will become sparklingly clean without the kit ever seeing the washing-machine. Then, as a last-minute gift on the actual day of the match, they clean their football boots in my sink, leaving clods of grass and mud to block up the plughole. Of course this behaviour is unreasonable, and they have of course been told not to do it, and of course I tell them off, but it's *how* I do it. Rarely do I manage a reasonable and controlled response. I'm more likely to scream and rant and cry and behave as though the end of the world as we know it has come. When I am like that, I say things to them that are desperately unkind and aimed at reducing them to nothing. How can I do this when I love them so much?

Well, that rules out the next bit you said before I even come to it, doesn't it? 'Ill-mannered, selfish and irritable'. Yes, I'm all those. Probably at least once a week. Then there's, 'Love does not keep a record of wrongs.' But I do. I'm quite likely to throw every wrong thing they've ever done at them when I really get going. I've always hated bullying but I think that's what I do when I get going. I bully them. I use my power to shove them down, so that they are, at least for a moment, smaller and weaker than me.

I hang on to the rest of what you say. I do 'hate evil' and I do 'never give up' but I worry so much that I have failed them in keeping them safe from evil influences. I know they lie to me sometimes and don't tell me the whole truth about what they do and who they meet when they are not at home. Sometimes I feel that I believe in them but I don't believe them. Do you know what I mean, Paul? I think I do have faith that God loves them, but I worry he might not like them very much because sometimes I wonder if I do. I mean, how can I treat them so badly if I really like them so much? I do have hope for their future, so I do believe in them and their abilities to learn how to overcome, but I don't actually believe everything they say! Does this make me a realist or a suspicious, untrusting nasty?

You seem to have sorted your life out so well. You say, 'When I was a child my speech, feelings and thinking were all those of a child; now I am a man I have no more use for childish ways.' But I don't feel I have put away childish things. I feel as though I still respond to life like a big silly kid, as though at the age of 39 I'm still waiting to grow up.

Jill

Dear Jill

I think you sound a very nice person but also an extremely ungrateful one. No, I am not about to increase your guilt by suggesting that you count the blessings you have in the form of your children, your husband and your friends. Nor am I going to add to your sense of failure by suggesting that you should be happier with your situation. But I am going to challenge you on your lack of appreciation for the very considerable gift the Holy Spirit has chosen to bestow on you.

As I understand it, present-giving has always been an essential part of British celebration. Whether it is Christmas or Easter or a birthday or anniversary, gifts are exchanged. Judging from the lack of confidence displayed in your letter I would imagine that choosing gifts for your family takes a considerable time, partly because you will not trust your judgment, but also, I suspect, because you always try to choose the gift most suitable for each person. You think about their preferences in terms of colour and style, but you also think about equipment they might lack, things which would make their daily living more effective and enjoyable.

Dear Jill, the Holy Spirit loves you at least as much as you love your family. He looked at you and knew exactly what present to give you, the one most suited to you, the one which would enable you to fulfil your natural potential. There is no difference between 'charismatic' and 'non-charismatic' gifts. *All* of them are charismatic. All of them stem from the grace of God (which is what 'charismatic' means), including the greatest gift of all, the charisma of eternal life which every single one of his children automatically receives at the moment of their spiritual birth. Some of his gifts were—and are— practical, enhancing a natural bent towards hospitality or caring for the less fortunate. Some of them help the more academically minded to fulfil their potential as teachers and administrators. Apostles and evangelists, healers and miracle-workers may have appeared more spectacularly honoured, their gifts perhaps wrapped in showier paper, but I need hardly tell you how highly Jesus valued those who put the needs of others first, and how much he needed the friendship and support of those gifted in hospitality.

You say I practically converted the world, which is, if you don't mind my saying so, just a bit of an exaggeration, even allowing for the fact that the known world was somewhat smaller then than it is now. But I cannot imagine how I would have accomplished anything at all without the gift to me of dear friends and supporters who cared for me throughout my working life. I mean people like Priscilla and Aquila, my fellow tentmakers, who not only put up with me for months at a time when I was stationed in Corinth, but even accompanied me on my journey to Syria. Can you imagine how lonely and dispiriting life sometimes was for me? Sharing all my hopes and worries with this lovely couple kept me sane and singing. I was blessed with so many good friends, but it occurs to me as I write this that the special gift of putting others' needs before your own has always been rather expensive for those who receive it! Gaius and Aristarchus, who were my travelling companions from Macedonia, were seized by rioters and taken to the ampitheatre in Ephesus, while Silas, Barnabas and Timothy must have sometimes questioned the generosity of the Holy Spirit, bearing in mind beatings and imprisonments from the enemies of the Way, and the grumpiness and stubborness of one of the chief advocates of the Way, namely myself!

Then, of course, there was Luke. My dear friend Luke, so dependable, discerning and thoroughly good. He was such a learned man, a wonderful writer and a superb doctor and yet, did you know that when I was an old man, stuck in jail in Rome, waiting to be executed, my beloved old physician was there with me, loyal to the very end?

Jill, I'm sure you are wondering why I am going on and on about myself and my friends when you have written so graphically about what seem to you insurmountable failures. Well, it is because I want you to be a little more appreciative of what you have received from the Holy Spirit. I think I am going to have to thank him on your behalf. First, I am going to thank him for giving you a present which has preserved you from some of the silly abuse which can accompany the showier gifts. It was in my beloved, but often extremely annoying, church in Corinth where the silliest excesses occurred. They were such an egocentric crowd and they failed to understand that the more overtly mystical gifts were intended to be shared with the whole church just as much as the practical gifts. You see, the Holy Spirit must have decided that Corinth needed a lot of help because he showered them with presents. Prophecy, discernment, faith, tongues. You name it, someone in their church got it! If everyone had shared the gifts as the Spirit intended, the church would have been incredibly rich. It should have been wonderful, but it wasn't, because they didn't care enough about each other. Instead, they behaved like naughty children in class whose teacher has turned her back to write important information on the board—babbling away in tongues all at the same time, and not bothering to listen to what God was trying to teach them. It was to them that I wrote the piece which you said was used at your wedding and to them that I spoke about putting away childish things, not to people like you who are already grappling with the difficulties of trying to walk the Way of love. Of course it's hard, and of course you fail. There was only ever one who managed it successfully. But even he needed friends, and I thank him that he has called you to support him. Oh, yes, Jill. Do you not remember what he said? Whatever you do to care for the least of his brothers and sisters, you do for him.

Now, this is the point where I am going to get a bit stern with you. You don't seem to me to be sufficiently appreciative of the honour bestowed upon you. You may feel that your house isn't tidy, but people keep walking through your door to ask you for help, don't they? Does it ever occur to you, in your panic about the washing-up, that God may have sent them? Do you ever wonder why he has sent them to you? Hardly in order for you to impress them with your housekeeping. How is *that* 'giving God a good reference'? He isn't a manufacturer of washing-machines, is he? He has sent his lame and his suffering to you because you are one of the team he has especially equipped for the task of listening and caring. You may not feel that you have useful Bible verses at your fingertips or eloquent prayers in your head, but you have been told to ask the Holy Spirit to give you the verses or to pray for you. Your gift is given to you so that God, through you, can build his Church. Of course he wants you to ask 'What Would Jesus Do?' but he needs you to let him get involved so that he can show you by example what he will do! If you don't, then you could be in as much danger of abusing your gift as the tongues-babblers were in Corinth.

Jill, I have deliberately been stern because you are one of God's frontline workers in the war against the evil one, whose sole purpose is to separate human beings irrevocably from the love of their heavenly Father. You are right when you say that you need to put away childish things, but you are not right in your assessment of what they are. Worrying about the times when you are not loving towards your family is not the childish thing you need to put away. It needs sorting out with God's help, not throwing away. No, the rubbish you have believed since you were a child about the need to achieve on your own is what needs to be thrown out, and as soon as possible, please. You say you want to be a more effective witness. Now you know how. The Holy Spirit needs you back as soon as possible, fit for duty.

Your fellow soldier in Christ,

Paul

~ Jerry ~

Dear Paul

I am delighted to finally make the acquaintance of someone who, unbeknown to him, is currently playing such a prominent role in my life! Let me explain.

For 31 years I have enjoyed life without any major complications whatsoever. I am blessed with being that rather archetypal English-woman, the 'good all-rounder'. At school I tended to come in the top three to six for just about everything from PE (junior long-jump county record holder for three years running) to art. I was a competent tennis player, played the cello to grade six, and was house captain. I was also captain of the inter-schools debating society. Without too many ripples I made it into Sheffield University, had a wonderful three years there, apart from one small hiccup of a loved but lost boyfriend, and bounced out with a 2:1 in History and English joint honours. During the time I was there, I continued to play sport reasonably competitively, was on the board of the uni union and joined the debating society and also the choral society. I made some wonderful friends over the three years, and I think it would be true to say that the letters J.G.S. (Jolly Good Sort) could have been added to my G.A.R. (Good All-Rounder) alongside my B.A. Hons! I've remained in touch with several of those friends and one is responsible for your entering my life and my subsequent confusion.

About nine months ago, he phoned me to say that there was a new choral society starting in the town where he worked, about seven miles from where I now live. He was thinking of joining. What about me? He suggested we went for a pizza afterwards. Well, you know me —well of course you don't!—but anything for a free meal! So I went, but it turned out to be rather an elderly bunch and I decided it wasn't for me long-term. But I did agree to boost their altos at a sort of pre-Christmas community carol service in the town's leisure centre.

When I got there for the compulsory practice at about 6.30, I was somewhat dismayed. Not only was the borrowed navy formal dress about three sizes too big for me, but I found we were sharing the small makeshift stage with the local brass band, tubas and trombones included. It was extremely hot and squashed and quite frankly pretty disorganized. There were young people everywhere, stringing fairy lights from wall bars and putting programmes on seats, and there was a veritable army of small children dressed as angels, shepherds and so on munching through enormous packed teas, while their mums attempted to fix tinsel hairbands on slippery, newly washed hair. 'One-two-threes!' were booming and crackling from the several microphones rigged up in front of the stage and, to be honest, by the time it was due to start I was feeling thoroughly irritated with the whole thing and wishing I'd simply slipped out before the jamboree began. In a way, I still wish that, but for different reasons.

You see, in the middle of the Christmas readings, the brass band, our slot and a somewhat inaudible children's nativity play, I was ambushed. I, who had always been so proud of being in complete control of my life; who had always adopted the popular Marxist view towards the whole question of religion (you know, opium of the masses and all that jazz). I, who had started the evening refining my Christmas present list in my head, somehow allowed my defences to be lowered and something to creep up on my heart and capture it. That's honestly how it felt. I looked round at the sports hall brimming with people of all ages singing with their hearts hanging out of their mouths and, instead of feeling the derisory reaction I was used to experiencing when I happened to catch *Songs of Praise* on the telly, I found myself wanting to feel how they felt. On the way home, I gave myself a good shake and told myself it was just a reaction to the tinsel and sentimental associations of the traditional carols, but the feeling was still there in the morning and the next one and the next. I quietly took myself off to midnight mass on Christmas Eve at our local parish church and found myself weeping buckets behind the holly and ivy pillar decoration. Christmas Day was odd. It felt as if I was there but not there—as though there was a kind of invisible veil between me and everyone else. The nearest I can get to describing it is the way I felt during the early days of the 'loved but lost' period at university.

Clearing out my handbag the following week, I came across the programme for the carol 'do', and saw that it had a sort of advert for the church that claimed to have organized the whole thing. Apparently it met every Sunday morning in a junior school just nearby. The next Sunday saw me, guess where! I crept in the back after they had started and was, quite frankly, bowled over. There were about four hundred people dancing about, singing their heads off, and instead of laughing the whole thing out of court, I joined in— quietly, and at the back, but I did join in. We sang about how beautiful Jesus was and is and how his love had streamed through history. We asked him to change us, to make us new. For the first time in my life I wanted to be different. I opened myself up to being changed. I think—forgive me if you think I'm quite mad—I fell in love with the whole thing. Everything I heard about Jesus that week and over the next few weeks filled me with utter amazement that I had never heard of it all before. How could I possibly have got through 31 years without knowing these feelings, unaware of what my life cost Jesus?

Then, after I'd been going to this church for about five weeks, I was invited to join a sort of induction course which was compulsory if I wanted to become a member of the church. I was delighted, and bounded off to my first meeting like a puppy going to its first obedience class. That was where I met you. Oh, Jesus was there too, of course, but whereas he seemed to be offering me promises of fulfil- ment, security and joy, all you seemed to offer was discipline and condemnation. I discovered that, although the church I was in did not consider themselves extreme fundamentalists, nevertheless I could never be considered suitable for any leadership role except that of teaching children (hardly my forte!) I could not lead prayers from the front, preach, or run a housegroup, and I could never ever aspire to being part of what they called 'the eldership', a committee that ran the church. All the stuff about marriage roles wasn't immediately relevant, of course, though it still made me fume, but the limited role of women in the active running of the church quite frankly amazed me. And it seemed as though every time I incredulously demanded to know who could possibly have said that, the answer was you. I tried saying that surely then was then and now was now, but they were not able to see what my problem was. I'm still there, but I'm finding it more and more difficult to stay stuck in and to keep my mouth shut.

So Paul, what can you say to me? Is it really true that all my gifts of communication and all my training in management can't be used simply because I am a woman? How can I submit to such an archaic regime? I really am not a militant feminist, you know. I am a normal, balanced, reasonable, reasoning human being who just happens not to be male! Never has this made the slightest difference to the opportunities life has presented me with until now.

Answer me this one thing, Paul. If you were here today, would you still have established the same guidelines? And please, Paul, do me a favour, try to pretend I'm a man when you reply and treat me as an equal!

Yours,

Jerry Tate

Dear Miss Tate

Greetings in the name of Jesus to my new sister in Christ. May I express my joy that you have had the courage to challenge me so directly. I have always enjoyed debate with educated opponents and I have a feeling you will prove to be no exception. I will attempt to explain some of the areas which are clearly bothering you and hope that, at the end, you will at least have a clearer idea of what to argue against next time you meet with your elders!

However, I have no intention of pretending you are a man, for two very important reasons, which I will identify. The first is that to do so would undermine my acknowledgment of your equality and I would not want to go against everything I stood for while I was in the world. You praise unreservedly our Lord Jesus Christ. I did too. I, like you, was overwhelmed by his promise of fulfilment, security and joy. As a new Christian, though, I was as challenged as you have been by some of the things I heard about. You are—what were your words?—'utterly amazed'. Well, I was too. I was utterly amazed to hear from his friends about perhaps the most revolutionary fact of Jesus' earthly ministry, his dealings with women. I was a child of my time just as you are a child of yours. In my century, women were subordinate and considered inferior to men in every sphere of their lives. They had no real place outside the home and no power except within the home. They were commonly regarded as being lazy, garrulous, stupid, vain, frivolous and even morally dangerous. I'm sorry, but it's true. Men had a duty to clothe, feed and maintain their wives, but only in exactly the same way that they had a duty to their slaves. In law, women had the same lack of rights as slaves and did not receive the necessary education to change this, as they were considered unteachable! Jewish schools were open to boys and men only and the temple had a court set apart for the women.

It was into this cultural background that Jesus was born, and it was against this background that he impacted both the men and the women with whom he came into contact. Jesus saw women, for the first time, as individuals responsible for their sins, capable of repentance, with needs, gifts and failings. He healed them, touched them, talked to them, listened to them, and allowed them to touch him, to follow him, befriend him and serve him. Even his teaching and his stories related to women's issues as frequently as they did to those of the men, showing his respect for their spiritual insights and their need to learn more. For the first time, men and women were encouraged to relate to each other in a way other than specifically sexually. Nor was there any possibility of this failing to continue after his death. The angels announced the news of the resurrection to women, and it was left to them to inform the men. So from the very first days of the Christian Church, a radical new order had begun. From those first days in the upper room, women prayed with men, received the Holy Spirit, and were accepted fully into the membership of the Church. They were able to pray, prophesy and join in decision-making in ways hitherto unknown in Judaism. I came to all this without the experience of being one of Jesus' band while he was here, and I acknowledge that it was difficult to move from a Jewish to a Christian view of women without problems. I will, however, attempt to put before you evidence of my teaching which supported the radical example of our Lord.

I taught a fundamental doctrine to all my churches that there was no division in Christ—that men and women were equal in God's sight and, even more, that they were joint heirs to the kingdom. Any difficulties I had (and incidentally, Peter struggled as much as I did in putting the example of Jesus into practice) were matched by the inward struggles of the men in our churches, as they had to learn not to regard their wives in terms of their legal position, which was weaker, but their spiritual position, which was equal. But it was absolutely crucial that this was understood. All, men and women, were sinners standing in need of salvation. All were eligible for that salvation. All had equal access to the Father in prayer and shared the indwelling of the Holy Spirit. All were part of the priesthood of all believers, having equal access to public worship and the chance to live in a state of religious dedication. The body of Christ, one of my favourite and, I considered, most useful ways of describing the Church, consisted of male and female. Women did not belong to the Church. They *were* the Church, just as the men were. I am sorry to labour the point, but it is crucial for you to understand how revolutionary such ideas were. My habit of writing my letters to both men and women helped to reinforce the message, as the norm up till then had been for all moral treatises to be addressed to the men, allowing them to pass on such information as they considered appropriate.

Having said all this, being equal in God's sight does not make men and women the same. And that is the second reason why I would feel it inappropriate to pretend that you are a man. I refer not only to myself, but to all the earliest apostles when I say that we wanted women to understand that they didn't have to compete with the men in order to be free. They already were free in God's eyes. One of our greatest crises blew up in our volatile church in Corinth, where there was enormous confusion about whether or not women should abandon the custom of 'covering', when they came forward to pray or prophesy in the church. I had to remind them quite firmly that there was absolutely no need for them to concern themselves with outward appearances of equality, and therefore it was right and proper for them to continue in the tradition. Did you not in recent years go through a period when women felt it necessary to dress in a way denoting power, to emphasize their emancipation? It was much the same in Corinth. They had to learn that there was no need to compete, no need to strive. A woman should exercise her freedom to prophesy as a woman and a man as a man. And before I hear you say, 'What about your comments on marriage?' let me just remind you that submission is different from obedience. Children are asked in my letters to obey their parents. Wives are asked to submit voluntarily to their husbands and husbands to their wives. This is not simply splitting hairs, it is fundamental to understanding the difference between Christian relationships and those in our Greco-Roman Jewish world, where wives lived under the authority of their husbands with no right to choose how to behave at all. On the surface, not all that much had changed. I asked for women to behave in a decorous way, never domineering over their husbands or attempting to instruct them. I asked that they should voluntarily put their husbands' will and desires first. However, in asking men to care for the whole well-being of their wives, I was paving the way for an understanding of basic human rights which has been a part of our culture from then to now. In elevating the wife's role within the household to master of the house (*oikodespoteo*), I was ensuring that decision-making and ruling were no longer the sole prerogative of the husband, and by speaking constantly to both husband and wife in the same context, I was establishing a deliberate precedent.

There are three reasons for my insistence that the *status quo* within marriage and within the Church should appear essentially the same as before the time of Christ. The first is that, rightly or wrongly, I believed that there is an order which God established at the time of creation. Men and women were created with distinct differences. Adam was created first and then Eve. Woman was created from man who was therefore her source, just as God is the source of Christ. Therefore I had no difficulties with the concept of man having a protective, patriarchal role over his wife, especially as our Lord Jesus had turned the idea of leadership so firmly on its head. The headship of Christ meant his total self-giving and our salvation. To lead was to serve. That was the way I tried to live my life as leader, pastor and teacher, and that was the way I expected men to behave towards their wives. I specifically used the word *agapate* when referring to the kind of love I expected to see from Christian husbands—a serving love that would enable a wife to grow in her faith and confidence.

The second was an attempt to minimize the sociological problems developing from my preaching—preaching which negated the values of a society based on sexual, racial and social differences. You may accuse me of cowardice, but before you do, examine my final reason.

The third reason was to keep the reputation of the Church as clean as possible. This was vitally important to me. I did not consider that my first priority was to create a new social order but to preach the cross, itself an unpalatable message for a culture where only ambition and success were considered worthy of praise. I was anxious that the relative freedom of Christian women shouldn't give an impression of licence. You see, I remembered all too well how unimpressed I had been by the very earliest groups of followers who met in Solomon's porch at the temple in Jerusalem, and seemed so undisciplined and ignorant. I wanted the women of the Church to adorn the doctrine of our God and Saviour, not detract from the message in any way. I did not want anything to impede the spread of the gospel and I felt that further emancipation of our women might do just that. Now, you may argue that what I had to say about women in the Church is impeding the spread of the gospel in *your* lifetime. You may not think I was right, but all I can say is that my letters were written to meet the specific need of a specific group at a specific time. They were not intended as a model for the Church in another part of the world in another time. How could they have been? I thought the world was coming to an end in my lifetime!

What I would say to you is that the essential truths can be tested against time because they come from God. The specific details cannot be applied in the same way. All but Christ is conditional. When the church began in Jerusalem they shared everything they had. That wasn't the pattern I later established in my ministry, although I encouraged them to give generously and to look after groups such as widows who were unable to fend for themselves. Why? Because it no longer felt appropriate. At the point when I began my ministry, God's time was, of course, exactly right for the conversion of the Gentiles, a fact that one can see clearly only in hindsight. It was right partly because of the enormously increased ease of access from country to country. The seas were at last safer from bandits and the roads were passable and relatively fast. It was also right because of the new world order created by the spread of the Roman Empire.

The role open to women in the churches reflected the differences in culture of the area where they had been established, as much as they reflected my convictions. The Greco-Roman world was socially and culturally in a state of flux as these two very different cultures came together for the first time. The role of women, within the worlds of both marriage and work, was beginning to change. Many women were receiving education. There were increased economic rights over inheritance and in divorce, and some women were even beginning to travel with their husbands and have some influence in local governing of the Roman colonies. My early European churches reflected this increased flexibility, while the Christian church in Jerusalem was more traditional.

Mind you, this did not mean a relaxation in the need for women to be decorous, because the new order was bringing with it increased moral laxity and corruption and it was, of course, essential that this was not allowed to infect the church. What it did mean was that women were taking a more active role in church life in the churches of Europe. My dear friend Priscilla is a good example. She and her husband, Aquila, travelled and worked together as tentmakers and, apart from being my very good friends, they helped instruct Apollos in the faith, thus setting the church in Ephesus on excellent foundations. Together they led a house church, were fellow missionaries with me and even risked their lives for me. Together and jointly they were responsible for the building up of several of the early European churches. In Rome, several women were deeply involved, while the first church in Philippi was actually founded by a group of Jewish women after Lydia had accepted the Lord into her heart. Such a wonderful story of what God can do through women, Jerry. You see, there was, as yet, no synagogue for the Jews and the women used to meet down at the riverside when they went to do their washing. Therefore, just as the very first person to see the risen Christ was a woman, so the very first European Christian was a woman.

Then there were the women involved with the running of my church in Philippi. If I could do so, I would erase my references to

Euodia and Syntyche's rows because they give a very unfair picture of the valuable contribution these women made as my staunch allies in the work of spreading the gospel. And then, of course, there was Phoebe, an outstanding worker for God who took responsibility for running my daughter church in Cenchreae. I had no problem in working alongside women in my missionary work and no problem in allowing women to take a major part in the work of the Church where that was possible without causing offence.

So where does that leave us, Jerry?

Yours,

Paul

Dear Paul

It leaves me utterly bewildered and even more angry with my church. Are you in fact saying that I should, on the basis of what you wrote, be able to lead, pray, prophesy and preach? If so, then I am looking forward to a meeting with the elders that I have set up for next Friday.
  Yours,

Jerry

Dear Jerry

Now we come to perhaps the more difficult area of my thoughts and rules about the role of women in the Church. I am not going to beat about the bush with you, Jerry. I believed that it was inappropriate for women to take on one area of ministry, namely overall leadership and the preaching to and teaching of men. I know this is going to make you, with your background in communication studies, very angry. I am not going to defend what I believe to have been right for my churches but I will explain my reasoning. I have already said that the everyday running of the church was open to both men and women, and that women could pray and prophesy in the churches where that was not going to cause a scandal, such as in Caesarea where, I remember, Philip's four daughters all prophesied. However, at that time I did not envisage the possibility of women elders. The very name 'elder' may give you a clue as to why not. The elders— bishops—of my churches were older men in the congregations who would naturally, because of their education and experience and wisdom, fit the role. I laid down some pretty tough guidelines as to the qualities I was looking for, and I have to say that this exempted a large number of men as well as all women. They were expected to be experienced Christians with a gift for teaching and a reputation for being good, hardworking, sober, kind and orderly. It was assumed they would be married (to one wife!) with a well-behaved and disciplined family. So why could this not apply to a woman? Jerry, there was absolutely no way the men would have accepted a woman dominating them, whatever I may have thought for or against the proposition. They were already, as I have explained, challenged by the concept of treating women as equals. It would be the equivalent of your minister announcing that from now on your church was to be led by a twelve-year-old. The reaction would have been similar and the Church would have been held up as an object of ridicule to the rest of the male-dominated world.

I have to say that there was more involved than just the reputation of the Church or the feasibility of introducing such a radical step. I believed that it was contrary to natural order for women to teach their husbands, and this would have been the case had they been able to preach in church.

Yours, in anticipation!

Paul

Dear Paul

So you did say it! Well, some of it, anyway. So, Paul, I challenge you, if you were here today, what would you say? Would you still, in the light of the fact that women have proved themselves equally educable and equally capable of running businesses, say that women couldn't preach?

Yours,

Jerry

Dear Jerry

Your challenge is reasonable, but not one that I am able to answer. As I said, I was a child of my time, an extraordinary time in which the spreading of the gospel to the Gentiles was God's chief desire for me. The most effective way of doing that as quickly as possible was always my priority. I prayed about areas where advice was sought or where difficulties presented themselves. Sometimes God advised me. If such an answer was not given to me, I used my common sense. I suggested that women should have opportunities to learn for the first time, I encouraged their participation in all aspects of church life, but I did not deem it appropriate for the furtherance of the gospel to give them full authority over men.

Now, what you are asking me is, given the fact that in your century women have been given the vote and acquired equal status in education and equal opportunities in the world of work, would I say the same things? Of course, I can't tell you that because I am not living in your world. I will just say one thing. If I had been chosen to live in your times, I would definitely have addressed this problem as well as many others—homosexuality; divorce; surrogacy; abortion; schisms in the body of the Church; attitudes to the elderly; discipline of the young. Your church would have presented me with at least as many sleepless nights as mine did. It is just possible that I would have had to look at the question of the role of women in the same way that I had to look at our most disturbing problem, that of whether it was right for our Gentile converts to undergo the rite of circumcision. The conclusion that I came to over that issue was that these men had been accepted by God and given the blessing of the Holy Spirit without going through a ceremony which would have been seen by them as mutilation, and would have prevented many of them from following the Way. Therefore I had to conclude that to impose an expectation of behaviour which belonged to another race in another time was not what God wanted for them. It would have had the effect of placing free men under the law. So maybe...

There are choices within the body, you know. Some of what I believe you call 'denominations' have decided that it is right for women to have more influence and indeed equal opportunities of leadership. Some have encouraged their women, despite their obvious equalities in other walks of life, to submit willingly as an act of service to their Lord. Some have felt it right to follow closely the guidelines laid down in my time. Some feel those guidelines to be directly ordained by God and therefore sacrosanct.

Perhaps the greatest difference is that women in your time have the opportunity to choose for themselves which regime they will submit to. I will watch your meeting with your elders with interest.

Jerry, I think I would have liked to have had you as a fellow worker. Stay true to yourself and work out your salvation, with God as your head (however you decide my Greek should be interpreted!)

God bless you and keep you in his light.

Your friend,

Paul

Ruth

Dear Paul

I am wondering whether you have any advice for me. I am a happily married woman aged 42. I have two children, aged 11 and 15. They are lucky enough to have two complete sets of fit and loving grandparents. We are reasonably comfortably off—my husband, Tony, has a good job. He teaches at our local further education college and I work part-time as a classroom assistant. My husband is a caring husband and father. So, you see, on the surface we have few problems.

Over the last couple of years, though, we seem to have done nothing but row at home, and the problem is that the reason for most of the arguments is church. You see, Paul, my husband does not come from a Christian background. I do. I was always taken to church as a child by my mother and father, and it never occurred to me that it would be any different for my children. My husband is usually a very tolerant man and, while the children were small, he was quite happy for me to take them every Sunday. I think he secretly rather liked a couple of hours' peace and quiet with the Sunday papers and endless mugs of coffee. But about a year ago, my daughter went on a Christian camp and had a really wonderful experience of the Lord. Well, when she came home, she was so excited that she couldn't stop talking about it and naturally expected her dad to be interested. After all, he's always been involved in everything else exciting that has happened to her. Nothing could have been further from the truth. He was furious—absolutely went ballistic—and blamed me for letting her go, the youth group leaders for exposing her to such nonsense and my daughter for being stupid and gullible enough to believe it. Unfortunately my parents got in on the act! My father tends to speak his mind rather, and he told Tony in no uncertain terms what he thought. Then he asked me, in front of both the kids, what I had expected, marrying a non-Christian against their advice.

Tony's parents (unfortunately, if you see what I mean) came out of it with flying colours, being totally besotted with both their grandchildren. They declared, 'If it makes our Laura happy, then where's the harm?' Somehow this hasn't helped! It's complicated everything even more by making my mother and me wonder if we should have said something to them at that point about the vital importance of the death of Jesus. So we felt guilty about that as well. To make matters worse, my opportunist eleven-year-old son, who has been finding church pretty boring for some time, seized the moment to declare that he was no longer going to go along with something he disagreed with. Tony seemed to see this as a minor victory of some sort and, of course, Nana and Grandad Stokes were there to say that if it made their Davy happy to stay away from church, then where was the harm!

So now Sunday mornings are quite horrible in our house. Davy seems to delight in wandering around the kitchen in a towel, talking about how much he's looking forward to a leisurely bath or playing computer games with his dad. My daughter seems to have lost all her joy. My husband hardly speaks to us and I go off to church feeling guilty all round. Guilty that our son is no longer with me—unlike most of my friends' boys—and also guilty that Laura no longer feels confident with her Christian friends because she isn't allowed by her dad to go on any outings with the youth group. And then she feels a misfit at school as well because she can't go with them to boot fairs or into town on a Sunday morning.

I know you never had children of your own but please, if there is any way you can help, let me know. My mum sends her love and says to say that your writing has helped her on numerous occasions and she just wishes she had your imagination and ingenuity to find a way to help our little family, which seems to be falling to bits before her very eyes.

Yours,

Ruth Stokes

P.S. I've just read this through and feel that Tony doesn't come out of it in a very nice light. Please don't get me wrong. He really is a very nice man and I love him dearly. In fact, and please don't refer to this if you write to me, he sometimes demonstrates a more Christian attitude than my dad, who is a bit quick off the mark where judging others is concerned! I can't help worrying that all this has put Tony off Christianity even more. I've always hoped that my faith would win him over for the Lord one day and now I feel that has all been ruined. Love,

Ruth

Dear Ruth

Greetings first of all to the tiny church situated in the middle of the Stokes family!

Before we look at the immediate problem, may I just say something to you that I said to 'mixed marriage' couples in Corinth. Their world wasn't so very different from yours. It was a fast-moving, aggressive, consumer-led society, where expediency and opportunism were the norm. It also advocated a very liberal attitude to morality. Did you know, for example, that one of the temples, the Acro-Corinth, was a temple to one thousand prostitutes. The sexual revolution didn't start in the 1960s, you know!

As you can imagine, I spent rather a lot of my time helping worried new Christians who were trying to live out their spiritual lives in the light of the permissive society they belonged to. Sometimes this meant reminding folk like your father of the need to build relationships with those outside the Church. I actually said at one point that if they followed their inclinations to have nothing to do with the contaminating influences of those outside the Church, they'd have to take themselves out of the world altogether! Judging from the letters I've received over the last few weeks, a lot of 21st-century Christians could perhaps do with a bit of my rather more forthright teaching on the subject of mixing the business of gospel living with the pleasure of sexual activity. But not you, my dear Ruth.

To you I want to say something else. Being a cosmopolitan city, Corinth inevitably saw many mixed marriages between Jews,

Gentiles and Christians. It worried believing partners just as much then as it worries you now. I made sure they understood that the opinion I offered then was a personal view. In other words, God had not told me to say it. But I based it on something Peter told me.

I urged them not to separate from their partners under any reasonable circumstances because I truly believed that an unbelieving husband was sanctified through the prayers of his wife and vice versa. Keep praying for Tony and try to trust God in this and in all things. The violence of his reaction to the irrational reminds me all too painfully of my over-zealous response to the apostles' insistence that Jesus, publicly crucified, with many witnesses to his death, was in fact alive and—more than that—the longed-for messiah. This should give you and me hope for Tony. To me, an educated Jew, this claim was nothing short of lunacy. The law was laid down in Deuteronomy and quite clearly stated, 'Anyone hung on a tree is under God's curse.' Crucifixion was the most degrading form of execution imaginable and these uneducated idiots were trying to tell me, an educated man of the world, that there was a glory in it! How ridiculous! To Tony, what has happened to Laura reeks of irrationality and offends what he sees as his modern scientific approach to life. He may even be associating what happened with cultism. He may feel hurt that what he saw as generous tolerance of your religion has been abused. It really doesn't matter, you know. Don't blame him for his response. Dear Ruth, pray with your mother for a meeting between your husband and his Lord, and rejoice that your daughter's experience has touched him so strongly. God can do a lot with passion!

Now on to the other matter worrying you—that of your children. How normal they sound! How lucky they are to be surrounded by so much love, even if it is causing problems at the moment. I am honoured that you seek my opinion at all. Reading your letter reminds me of my relationship with Timothy, who was like a very dear son to me. Actually, my reference to Timothy is more appropriate than you might think. Did you know that he himself was the son of a mixed marriage? Timothy's mother and grandmother were Jewish and his father was Greek. This was fairly acceptable socially at the time for Jews living outside Palestine, and the Greeks were known for their religious tolerance. In Lystra, where Timothy grew up, there were

Greeks worshipping their gods (including, for a few ludicrous hours, Barnabas and myself), native Lystrians worshipping their gods, and Jews worshipping God. Oh yes, Timothy's father was fashionably tolerant, but only up to a point, rather like Tony. He was quite happy to allow his wife and mother-in-law to teach little Timothy any amount of what he saw as harmless information from their scriptures, but he drew the line categorically at a Jewish name for his son. Timothy means 'honoured by the gods' in Greek. Moreover, he refused point-blank to allow his baby son to be circumcised. Oh, you can understand it from his point of view. The Greeks took such a pride in physical male beauty that this apparently meaningless ritual must have seemed positively barbaric.

But imagine what this must have been like for young Timothy as he grew up. For boys in Lystra, swimming and athletics took place in the nude and toilets were communal, so there was no hiding-place for his shame among other Jewish boys. He would have been considered not only unclean but also unblessed. On the other hand, the insistence of Eunice and Lois that he follow their God would have inevitably curtailed the freedom he might have enjoyed as a Greek. The lad must have felt, like your Laura, that he fitted nowhere.

Yet this insecure boy is the very person God chose out of all the young men growing up at the time to be my chief source of strength throughout my ministry, and a great evangelist and church leader in his own right. As I remember it, I do believe he was only in his thirties when he took the leadership of the troubled church in Ephesus under his gentle wing. Getting to this point involved Timothy gaining the courage to take a stand for what he believed, independent of both his mother and father. I visited Lystra while he was still what you would call a teenager. Both his mother and grandmother were converted to Christ, and with them was this boy, prepared to firmly proclaim Jesus as Lord in front of the many witnesses at his baptism.

I confess I don't remember much about them then—events got rather dramatic after I had been there for a short while—but I will never forget my return about a year later. As you probably already know, I spent a large portion of my working life rushing round the little new seedling churches with a spiritual watering-can, trying desperately to keep them alive and prevent any thorns from choking their delicate lives. Well, meeting Timothy again was one of those wonderful occasions where I realized that the chief gardener had been at work in my absence. He was not yet 20 years old, yet everywhere I went people were talking about the lad, even in Iconium, which was about thirty-five miles away. Make no mistake, even then he wasn't preaching an easy way. After all, the first time he had met me he'd seen for himself the down side of accepting Christ as his Saviour. Lois and Eunice may have had no difficulty reconciling my message with their Jewish scriptures but that didn't apply to many of the Jews in the area. In fact, a posse from as far afield as Antioch in Pisidia and Iconium pursued me to Lystra and succeeded in not only getting me thrown out of the city gates but also stoned almost to death. Oh yes, I was left for dead. Timothy was under no illusions about the probable cost of following Christ but he was also aware from the beginning of the power of the Holy Spirit. How else had I been able to get up on my feet and immediately go back into Lystra for another bout!

The personal cost for Timothy began early on in his walk. He too wanted to preach to both Jews and Gentiles, and who, you might think, bearing in mind his background, could be better suited? But it was to involve an immediate sacrifice, for I demanded that he must be circumcised before he could join me on my travels.

It must have been as bitter and bewildering a blow for Timothy as it was for Laura when Tony suddenly appeared to act so out of character. I must have seemed so stern and so unyielding. Not a dissimilar gauntlet to the one thrown down by Jesus to the wealthy young man, but potentially far more painful! Why? Why did I do it? Why did I risk losing this potential ally? After all, I had just come from a major debate in my home church in Antioch over whether new converts must be circumcised or not. Our case had been based on the way God had poured out his Spirit on new Gentile converts who had *not* first become nominal Jews by going through the sacrifice of circumcision. And we had won a resounding victory. So why did I ask so much of this young man who had already had to cope with so much distress during his short life? His father had died by then, by the way. It was because I knew and God knew that Timothy wanted in his heart to evangelize to both Jews and Gentiles, and that the Jews who knew his father was a Greek would otherwise never have listened to him.

One day, Laura will have to be brave. One day, her faith will be tested and she will have to decide, as Timothy did, whether she can risk stepping outside her father's approval and also cope with the inevitable teasing from her friends at school. Don't pray that the cup of suffering will be taken from her. Pray that you, your mother and she will have the courage needed when the time comes. And pray in earnest for young Davy. Pray that he will be kept safe from the evil one. Don't be tempted to emphasize the fun aspects of being in the Church. Don't lay your feelings of inadequacy as a Christian parent at his door. Remember Timothy. Pray that some day someone will walk into his life as I did into Timothy's to set alight the kindling that you have so carefully laid in his heart.

I know how hard it is to watch from the sidelines and feel helpless. I know how much we want to make life easy for those we love. But I want to say one last thing to you. It was Timothy's sensitivity and awareness of his unhealed wounds that was used by his heavenly Father to be such a support to me and such a light to so many Gentiles and Jews.

We are human. We all want to remove thorns from the flesh of those we love. But I had to learn that it is through our open wounds that the Holy Spirit can pour his healing. It was the same for our Saviour. By his stripes we were healed. So try to do the very thing I exhorted my dear 'son' Timothy to do. And encourage Laura to do the same. 'Take your part in suffering as a loyal soldier of Christ Jesus.' Remember that your being in chains might be the very thing that releases the good news to those you love.

Give my warmest greetings to your mother. Tell her that I thank God for her faithfulness in bringing you up as a child of God. Tell her to ask the Holy Spirit for one or two little aids in the imagination and discernment departments.

May the grace and the love of our Lord Jesus Christ be always with you.

Paul

~ *Thea* ~

Dear Paul

It gives me great pleasure to take this opportunity to tell you what I think of you. First of all, as a woman, I find your arrogance and coldness two of the worst male traits. You seem to see yourself as a cut above all other mortals and even above the law. How can anyone have the audacity to say, 'I care very little if I am judged by you or by any human court, indeed I do not even judge myself. My conscience is clear'. And don't pretend you never said it because you did, at the beginning of one of your ghastly letters to the poor normal people struggling to live out their oppressed lives in Corinth. How you, of all people, can say your conscience is clear after murdering goodness-knows how many innocent Christians is beyond me. This extraordinary arrogance spills over into everything else you pontificated about. Do you realize that, because of your misogynistic views, women have been repressed throughout history? Because of your complete indifference to the glaring injustice in the society you lived in, slavery was considered acceptable until a somewhat more compassionate individual than yourself, William Wilberforce, actually bothered to do something about it in the 19th century. As a historian, I am personally ashamed of the way missionaries, following your wonderful example, have trampled over the national identities of every underdeveloped country they could lay their greedy little hands on.

Oh yes, I could point out that I am a history teacher in a comprehensive school in Brixham, but no doubt that would fail to impress you, seeing as you say you will destroy the wisdom of the wise and frustrate the intelligence of the intelligent. Also, most of the children I teach are of such a low social class, no doubt you will tell me that I'm wrong to encourage them to fight their way out of their cultural ghetto. Do you realize how hard it is for the young people I teach to break through the barriers of sex, race and class imposed by this so-called Christian society? Do you take any responsibility for laying down the ground rules of this repressive religious regime which has dominated the Western world for two thousand years? Do you? Will you stand trial in my court? Will you defend yourself against the just accusations I am throwing at you on behalf of the children I attempt to educate and set free from the chains you and your successors have placed on them? To say smugly, 'My conscience is clear' is not enough in a 21st-century court of law. You have to answer the charges made against you.

I am not expecting you to respond, as I would imagine you will consider it completely beneath you to condescend to reply, but at least *my* conscience is now clear!

Yours faithlessly,

Disgusted of Brixham

Dear writer

I confess to being taken aback by the force of anger you are directing, not only at myself, but apparently at everything I wrote and did and, indeed, stood for. I found your tone hurtful and aggressive. You ask me to take my place in a dock and defend myself. You were right in assuming I would refuse, but not right in the motives you ascribe to me in coming to that decision.

As I understand it, those accused of criminal activity in your 'so-called Christian' country have a right to a free trial and are considered innocent until proved guilty. Am I not also right in thinking that the guilt of the accused is decided by a randomly chosen jury of twelve members of the population who have to declare if they have any vested interest in the case? Any potential bias is ruled out by members of the jury being asked to stand down. It is the jury's verdict that will decide the future of the accused. You are asking me to stand before a kangaroo court where the judge and jury have already decided that I am guilty. I am not prepared to defend myself under such circumstances. As a citizen of Rome during my lifetime, I feel very strongly about rights. When I was alive and was falsely accused, I stood out for a fair trial and demanded that my case should be heard in the equivalent of the high court, which, in my case, meant travelling to Rome.

My second reason for refusing to enter into dialogue with you is that I am deeply dismayed by the superficial assumptions you have made about my contribution, or lack of it, to the social situation of the time I lived in. You say you are a historian. Does this not usually mean in-depth research, sifting of evidence and reasoned arguments based on documents of the time?

The third reason for not being anxious to 'come to your court' is that I found your letter to reek of the very characteristics you accuse me of displaying, namely arrogance and coldness.

If you really want to enter into debate with me, I am more than willing to do so as I did in every city I worked in. I'm afraid, Miss Disgusted, that the ball is very much in your court, and I don't mean a legal one. I await your reply with interest.

Yours sceptically,

Apparently Arrogant of Tarsus

Dear Paul

Having re-read my original letter which, fortunately, I still had on my computer, I find myself somewhat embarrassed. There is perhaps some justification in your accusation that I was angry and may have been rather aggressive in my approach. I would argue that this anger is righteous because I feel very strongly about the young people I work with, and sometimes feel I am the only one who really cares what happens to them. That doesn't mean that I retract any of the accusations levelled at you. I still think you have a case to answer. I have to confess, though, to finding your remarks about my historical perspective being clouded rather disturbing, because I have always prided myself on my analytical approach, and I can see that perhaps I was not putting this into practice as rigidly as I should have done. I will attempt to rectify my error of approach and be more open in my response if you will commit yourself to truthfully expounding your methods and take responsibility for what you have done. I can't guarantee I won't still get cross, but I will listen.

Yours,

Rather Less Disgusted of Brixham!

Dear young lady

I am delighted to hear that you are prepared to listen to what I have to say. I certainly do not expect you to accept it simply because I've said it, and would ask you to follow it up with further research of your own.

Before I begin, can I just say how glad I am that you have indeed chosen to work among the disadvantaged in your society and that you are involved in trying to improve their chances? Now, the first difficult thing that I want to challenge you with is the idea that, contrary to what you suggest, I too was directly involved in trying to improve things for those less advantaged sections of the populations I encountered. The second thing I would like to put before you is that I did so not from a position of superiority but because I considered myself to be the lowest of the low and was deeply grateful to have been chosen to serve my Lord as his ambassador. The third thing is that I abhor, as much as you do, the appalling effects of some Western missionary attempts to impose their own cultural norms on primitive societies under the banner of Christianity. That was not what Christ intended and it is not what I myself practised. If you would like me to expand on any or all of these points, let me know.

Yours,

Paul

Dear Paul

While I try to keep my cool, and restrain my impulse to laugh, could you tell me first of all how you can equate what you said about marriage with what I said about trying to improve the status of my disadvantaged teenage girls? You were very explicit in what you had to say about women's role within marriage. 'Wives must submit completely to their husbands just as the Church submits itself to Christ', and again, 'A husband has authority over his wife.' I know you weren't the only one. I know that Peter said it as well, but in a way, that strengthens my argument that the rules laid down by the early Christian Church were responsible for the inequality which has favoured men over women right up to the century I live in. Women have been owned by their husbands, symbolized until recently by the dowry given by the father of the bride to the groom, and more recently by the bride's father paying for the wedding and by the ring the woman is given in the marriage ceremony. In the past, women have had no rights, no financial independence and they have been unable to divorce. What can you possibly have to say in mitigation? I really am interested to hear your reply.

Yours,

Thea Downing

Dear Thea

At last, something that moves this debate on to a slightly higher plain than mere personal insults.

Can I start by assuming that, as you haven't mentioned it, you are unaware of the position held by women in the first century? You appear to be suggesting that we imposed a more repressive role on women than that to which they were accustomed, or, at the very least, that we supported and encouraged the continuation of evils already present. I would contend that we did in fact bring about some radical improvements in the position of married women. But we did this through the men. We hoped desperately, in the light of the glorious new truth that under Christ all were equal in the sight of God, to convince men of the vital importance of women and children to their heavenly Father. It was not going to be easy.

Do you know that every morning Jewish men thanked their God that he had not created them 'Gentile, slave or woman'? Do you know that in Jewish law a woman was considered just one of her husband's possessions, to do exactly what he wanted with, including throwing her away if he so wished. Divorce, by the time I was born, had become incredibly easy. The clause in the Law of Moses which had become so open to abuse was the one stating that if the wife 'finds no favour in his eyes because he has found some indecency in her, he writes a bill of divorce and puts it in her hand and sends her out of his house'. 'Finds no favour' had been interpreted by one or two rabbis to mean that if the husband 'fancied' (the current word in your language, I believe) another woman more than his wife, he could divorce her. 'Indecency' had moved equally far from its original intended definition of adultery to include walking in the street with her head uncovered or having a row with her mother-in-law. Not a very good reason to find yourself out on the streets with a bill of divorce signed by your husband's rabbi in the presence of a couple of witnesses.

Women, by contrast, had no rights whatsoever, unless their husband became engaged in some utterly revolting trade or caught leprosy. 'Oh yes,' I can hear the prosecution saying, 'but that was the Jews. You were writing to Europeans, imposing your rules on a society renowned for its religious tolerance and its cultural sophistication.' Well, let me put one or two more facts before the jury. Did you know that in Greece a personal prostitute was considered an essential little luxury that no Greek husband should be expected to do without? His wife was there for the purpose of having legitimate children and running the house. Practically a prisoner in her own apartment, which only her husband could enter, she would never even appear at meals or at any public event or social occasion. In fact, as Xenophon put it, it was intended by Greek husbands that the wife should 'see as little as possible, hear as little as possible and ask as little as possible'. What is more, the husband didn't even need a rabbi's signature to enable him to divorce his wife for whatever reason he chose.

It was into this totally male-dominated culture, where fidelity in marriage was a joke, that I dropped my bombshell of expectation for men in a Christian marriage. Oh yes, it is true that I still asked women to submit to their husbands but it is in the demands I placed on European men that I showed my teeth. You accurately quote my remarks on women. Unfortunately, you totally misinterpret them and, what is more, you completely ignore what I said to men. Please look at my letter to the churches in Asia Minor again.

Before I move on to my remarks to married women, is it not true that I ask both partners to submit to one another? I ask men (and remember, I am speaking to European men who held physical male beauty in high regard) to love their wives as they loved their own bodies. To ask men to care deeply for their wives was radical indeed. What I was aiming at bringing about was a situation in marriage where service was lifted from being the married woman's domain, with minimal respect attached to it, to being an ideal to be sought by both men and women. In other words you could go as far as to say that what I was suggesting was the prototype for the 'new man' you and your women's liberation movements have fought so hard for. I rest my case!

Yours,

Paul

Dear Paul

Why is it I feel as though, somehow, you have squirmed your way out of that? I'm beginning to see how you managed to survive for so long! I put it to you, Paul, that whatever you may say now, you didn't personally like women—that my description of you as being a misogynist was based on remarks you made other than when you were speaking of marriage.

Yours,

Thea

Thea

I believe that at this point the lawyer defending my case would leap to his feet and cry, 'Objection, mi-lud!' and the judge would peer at him through what appears to be part of his uniform—his glasses on the end of his nose—and say, 'Objection sustained.'

We agreed to conduct this trial on issues other than personal opinions. If you want to know why I believed in the dignity of service, I will continue. If this is to descend into a conversation conducted at the level of what my favourite colour is, I request the right to withdraw.

Paul

Dear Paul

Please continue. But don't expect to bully me into believing you.

Thea

My dear Thea

The last thing I want to do is to bully you. Don't you see that that is the very essence of what I was trying to say in my day? I was urging people to put aside the ways of the world, the ambitions and greed which cause us to trample on one another. I was calling on people to be gentle and humble, patient and tolerant, to live sacrificially. We are all given different jobs to do for Christ. But all of those jobs have one thing in common: they are intended to serve, and, through that mutual service, to build up the body of Christ. The other thing they have in common is that each job is equal in God's sight. I have already mentioned the equal value of the roles of husbands and wives. This applied in my mind also to slaves and their masters. European men were used to bullying not only their wives but also their slaves. But they would not have seen this as wrong in any way, because slaves were not considered human beings at all, but tools—instruments of labour. As such, they were to be thrown away when old and rusty. In fact, the Roman law accepted that 'the master possesses the power of life and death over a slave'. It is to these most cruelly treated of men that I was speaking—and there were thousands of them in the early Church.

You say that I should have brought about abolition of the injustice. My contention is that I gave slaves a greater freedom than any that would have been produced by changes in the law. I let them know the amazing truth that they were as much heirs to the kingdom of God as their masters were—that they were equal in God's sight, and that Jesus died for them. I called them to recognize the freedom and value they had in their Father's eyes and to rise to the challenge of living a Christian life of dignified service where they were. Even when they were not being watched, I asked them to do the task in front of them beautifully, for their master, God, and I gave them equal responsibility with their masters for not bringing the name of God and our teaching into disrepute.

Social reform may bring about a far better standard of living for those at the lower end of our class systems, but only a genuine belief in one's personal worth will bring about equality. This I believe I brought, on behalf of a Lord who always looked out for the welfare of the least of his subjects. Incidentally, I did remind the Christian slave masters to remember that they and their slaves both belonged to the same Master in heaven. I think this just might have brought about better working conditions for the slaves, don't you?

Yours,

Paul

Dear Paul

It's all very well you saying all that, but the fact remains that slaves continued to be repressed for hundreds of years, women continued to be abused within marriage, and in some parts of the world these awful things still happen. I have in my school young Muslim women, already married in their teenage years, who are so totally owned by their husbands that they are not even allowed to show their faces out in the street; young West Indian women who have struggled against racist intolerance almost as cruel as the attitudes you ascribe to the slave masters; and young British women who have so little self-respect that they allow their bodies to be used by men. Nothing has altered, Paul, nothing. Why? Why hasn't Christianity brought about a complete change? Why do barriers still prevent all our young people from having the same chance in life?

Thea

Dear Thea

You are right, I am afraid. Evil has always been there and always will be until our Lord decides to return. In the early years of my ministry, I thought he was going to return really soon. That is what prompted some of my less tolerant outcries against things which, to me, seemed mere distractions from the task of bringing as many people to him as we could before he returned in judgment. I was wrong. Now, the only thing I know for certain is that I do not know when he will return!

In the meantime, barriers of race, religion and class continue to exist. Sadly, the natural desire to dominate has always created divisions and caste systems. You are also right that, in the past, missionaries have attempted to impose their own national or limited style of Christianity on the countries they evangelized. An even more deadly form of control developed from the misinterpretation of scripture by the Dutch Reform church when they settled in South Africa. I can only say that it was never God's purpose to create barriers, and much of my time was spent trying to break down those which were already in place. Before we go down the road we have just come from, that of social reforms, let me make it clear that the most dangerous barriers are those in the mind, and it was these that I addressed. Israel had always been set apart. 'Holy' actually means 'different', and the people of Israel believed that they were set apart from all other societies in the most fundamental way possible. Their king was God. He belonged to them exclusively. They alone had access to the inner courts of the temple. That is, until Jesus.

Did you know that in the temple in Jerusalem there were a series of courts, only the first of which could be entered by Gentiles. Between it and those reserved for the Jews was a marble screen which contained inscriptions to the effect that no foreigner could enter further on pain of death. And believe me, the Jews in my time took their rules seriously—so seriously that when I was myself accused, wrongly as it happens, of sneaking a Gentile friend, Trophimus, into the temple, I ended up with what eventually proved to be life imprisonment and subsequently my death!

Jesus Christ, through his death, crashed through this barrier as effectively as the famous breaching of the wall in Berlin. Gentile and Jew were declared equal in his sight: he belonged to them all and they to him. The good news that I had the task of imparting to as much of the world as I could was the all-inclusiveness of Christ. Male and female, slave and freeman, Jew and Gentile were all one. There was no longer to be a hierarchy when it came to having access to God. Jesus himself had made it very clear. 'All you have to do,' he said, 'is to go into your room, close the door and talk to your Father.' It was a radical message and, to many, a very unpopular one. People love barriers, Thea. They always have. Fences make them feel safe and secure.

Remember, the very first Christians were Jews—Peter, Matthew, John and James... and me. We were all Jews who came to believe that Jesus was our Lord and Saviour, but circumcised Jews, none the less. It needed a vision to convince Peter that God's love was to be spread to all nations. But we were used to hierarchies! It needed more than an apostle's vision to convince many new converts from Judaism that foreigners did not first have to become Jews through circumcision, before receiving forgiveness.

I did not always succeed, but I did try to communicate the idea that Christ altered both Jews and Gentiles into a totally new kind of person, the Christian-Jew and the Christian-Gentile. So none of the old rules need apply. Nowadays, thank goodness, I think that many of your missionaries have come eventually to understand what I was trying to say—that there can be Christian Africans and Indians who can enjoy their cultural differences but also be part of God's family with brothers and sisters of different classes and races. Jesus is our peace. I love him, and if you got to know him you would love him, and he loves us both. So we have that amazing thing in common. We can, if you want to, stand together in his presence because he has allowed both of us, from different cultures, different sexes and with our different ways of thinking, to do so. If we allow him to stand between us and look at each other through him, in some wonderfully mystical way our differences, while still being quite distinct, will fade into insignificance.

Thea, dear, may I just point out that the very fact that you were so quick to judge me suggests that maybe you, too, feel the need to create a barrier between yourself and the things you find threatening. Whatever your final judgment of me, please don't let your personal opinion be another barrier. Please give yourself the freedom to walk through the open gate in the fence and meet your Lord.

With love in Christ,

Paul

✒ Alison ✒

Dear Paul

Some of the things you say are a bit too hard for me to understand. You are so stern sometimes, and I don't think you are always very kind to people. But I do want to thank you for all the lovely nice things you say about love. They are so pretty and I have the 'whatsoever things' on my kitchen wall. My friend did it for me in her calligraphy class and it's decorated with birds and flowers and is really scrumptious. I also love the one about love from Corinthians which I've got on a bookmark in my Bible. It makes me feel really safe and happy when I read these lovely things. So I want to thank you that even though you were so clever and asked people to do such hard things in their lives, you also wrote things which were just nice and easier, if you know what I mean. I agree with you about looking only at nice things and don't ever let myself get into situations which could be nasty. I also think that to be nice to people is important and to animals too, although you don't mention them.

I have just started doing a cross-stitch picture of your 'Unto thine own self be true, it shall follow as the night followeth day thou shalt not then be false to any man', because I think that's really lovely too. It'll take me a very long time but I don't mind expending my energies on something worthwhile, any more than you did. I'm planning to do the 'P' of your name like they used to do letters in medieval Bibles, with gold thread. Thank goodness some of the things you said are nice enough for us to be able to give them to our non-Christian friends at Christmas as a Christian witness. I am going to give my cross-stitch to my friend Anna at work. She is a lot older than me and really nice, but she tells awful lies sometimes and keeps taking what she calls 'sickies' because she says things are a bit difficult at home. Of course, I haven't asked her what they are, as I think that would be rude. Oh, by the way, my very favourite of the things you wrote is *Desiderata*. If you were alive, I would ask you to write some more things like that, but as you are not I just want to say thank you and give you a big hug in love.

Yours,

Alison Moor

Dear Alison

I deeply regret to have to tell you that I am not responsible for writing either of the things you claim to be your favourites. I think that you need to be working out how to embroider a 'W' instead on your cross-stitch, as I believe the first passage you quoted was written by one William Shakespeare!

On a more serious level, I also have to tell you that I think you have been very misled in your Christian education. The things I wrote so urgently to my earliest churches about protecting their minds were in the context of living in the very centre of the world that you so obviously try very hard to avoid. The most serious error you make is to equate what I have to say about the value of love with something 'nice' and 'easy'. I feel you need advice and help in the areas of both living and loving, so I want to put you in touch with an expert who lives in your area. Her name is Jill Cotton and she lives at 27 Meadow Drive. I earnestly suggest you contact her as soon as possible before you bring the Christian message into serious disrepute.

I'm sorry to sound, as you put it, stern, but you are in danger of falling into grave sin. Christ himself had very stern things to say about the danger of causing little ones to stumble, and I feel you are in severe peril of denying your friend Anna the opportunity of finding access to the help of her heavenly Father and the Holy Spirit. I know that would not be your intention, as you are clearly very 'nice' yourself, and I am sure that with the right teacher you will fulfil your potential.

Just one thing. If you do decide to take up my suggestion to visit Jill, could you go armed not only with this letter but also with a packet of chocolate digestives and a can of Jasmine air-freshener. I know this makes no more sense to you than the vision given by God to Ananias instructing him go to Straight Street to lay hands on the most violent aggressor known to the first Christians. Trust me. This act of obedience will be the first of many important tasks the Lord has in store for you, once you have begun your discipleship training.

Yours,

Paul

✧ Andy ✧

Dear Sir

I'm sorry, but I don't know what to call you; and I feel a real idiot asking you what I am going to ask you, but I've got an essay to write for school about you, and I can't seem to sort something out. Are you Greek or Jewish or Roman? Someone even said you were Turkish! I've had a glance through Acts and you seem to keep changing your mind! The thing is, Paul, I haven't had much time—well, I know it's my fault because I've been playing too much cricket and I've left it till the last minute—but I've got my GCSE RE coming up, and I've got to get the essay in for my course work by the end of this week.

I don't expect you know this, but cricket is a game we play a lot with a bat and a ball, and GCSE is an exam we take when we're 16 here in England. I really need the answer tonight if it's not too much trouble. What I've gathered so far is that you wrote in Greek, you were a Jew and somewhere along the line you got out of trouble because you were a Roman. My mum and dad think I've already given in this work, so would you mind helping me stay out of trouble? I've got a hotmail address. I'm allowed an hour's surfing a day—that means being on the Internet. Oh heck, do you know what the Internet is? I hope so, because if you can use it they needn't know anything about it, need they? I am sorry to be a nuisance.

Please help if you can.

Andy

Dear Andy

I am quite happy to tell you the simple facts you need to know for your essay, but I expect you to tell your parents that I have helped you. If I could face the Christian community in Damascus and admit to them that I had been planning to have them put to death, I think maybe you can face your mother and father and tell them you have got behind with your homework because you have been playing too much cricket!

Right now, where shall I start? Your friend who told you I was Turkish is wrong, but I was brought up in Tarsus, which is part of what you would now call Turkey, so he wasn't so far out—except that then it was Greek! In fact, it was the centre of Greek culture as well as being the capital city of the Roman province of Cilicia and gateway to Asia Minor. One of its claims to fame is that Anthony met Cleopatra on the River Cydmus which flows through the city.

They didn't play cricket in Tarsus, but they were very much into sport, and they had one of the biggest athletics stadiums in the world. But I wasn't Greek. My family were Jewish through and through. You couldn't find a much more Jewish name than Saul, first king of Israel, and we were, in fact, descended from his tribe, the tribe of Benjamin. Have you heard of them? I rather suspect not! Anyway, I was circumcised when I was eight days old and grew up going to Jewish school and worshipping in the Jewish synagogue every Sabbath.

When I left school, I went to Jerusalem to study to become a Pharisee, which meant that I tried to keep all the laws of Moses every day of my life. So, as you can see, I was one hundred per cent Jewish. Having said that, I was also a Roman citizen and had, in fact, been one since birth. How? Well, because my father had been granted the privilege and all I had to do was inherit it!

Actually, I wasn't that unusual. By the time I was born, Rome had occupied most of the known world from the Atlantic Ocean on the west to the Euphrates on the east, and from the Danube and Rhine in the north to Africa and Arabia in the south. There were about six times as many Jews living outside Palestine as in it. So many of my race were living and working alongside Romans and there were lots of ways you could become a Roman citizen with all the privileges that went with it. You could join the army (not very common for Jews), you could buy your citizenship, or you could be awarded it for conspicuous service. Some of my own wider family have even got Roman names, Junia and Lucius being two of them. I opted for 'Paul', after the Roman Paullus, to mark my transition from Jew to Christian.

As a Roman citizen, you couldn't be subjected to the most degrading punishments (for example, crucifixion), and you had the right to appeal to the Roman Emperor himself. That came in extremely useful once or twice in my life, I can tell you! Especially once, when I had been thrown into prison and put into stocks with my friend Silas, and God had decided to let us go and laid on an earthquake which blew the locks to pieces! The magistrates were so scared that they told their officers to get rid of us as quickly as possible. I was able, calmly and truthfully, to tell them that as they had imprisoned us without trial even though I was a Roman citizen, they could jolly well escort us out themselves. You should have seen the faces of the magistrates as they accompanied us to the prison gates. It got me out of a flogging too, but that's another story and I can almost hear you saying, 'Get on with it, Paul, I've only got to write two hundred words!'

The last bit of the puzzle is correct. I did write in Greek, especially when I was writing to Greeks! No, seriously, because of Alexander the Great's conquests, Greek was spoken by everyone as well as whatever their native language happened to be—rather like your English language is spoken throughout the world today following on from your imperial days. Greek was the language of the Roman empire and the obvious language for Luke and me to write in. I once made a speech in Jerusalem in Hebrew, but the rest of the time I used Greek. Luke wrote one of the Gospels and also the book you call Acts, which you have been so gracious as to 'glance at'!

Just one last thing on the subject of citizenship, Andy. If you want to know how I considered myself, perhaps you might like to look into a letter I once wrote to my church in Philippi. You see, I wanted them to know the amazing truth that God had revealed to me, which was that we, as children of God, were no longer Greek or Roman or Jew but actually rightful citizens of another country altogether whose capital city was heaven. We simply had to put up with living out our temporary existence in this outpost we call the world, until we died and were able to go home.

Mysteries solved, Andy?

Paul

Dear Paul

Thanks for all the useful stuff you gave me. I did sort of own up to my dad about the cricket. Can't say he was very pleased. Can't say I think it was a very good idea. Still! Actually, I was wondering about one or two other things—not for an essay, honestly. The thing is, as I said, I'm doing RE (Religious Education). Well, as I expect you know, we don't just study Christianity, but all the religions. You name it, we do it! To be honest, Paul, I can't see a lot of difference between them. I mean, they all have a hero figure, they all have laws and festivals and rituals and sort of 'moral code' bits. They all stop their lot doing things and make them do other things. It sort of feels as if there's two sorts of people in the world, those who just want to have a good time and couldn't care less why they're here or where they're going when they die, and the other lot who search for some sort of meaning. But as far as I can see, we only think Christianity's good because we grew up with it in our country. I mean, if I lived in Turkey I'd be a Muslim, wouldn't I? I can't help feeling that they're all much of a muchness.

I know this wasn't a problem you had. You grew up being a Jew and swapped to being a Christian. But I've grown up going to church while some of my mates at school have gone to mosques or synagogues or whatever. Most of them didn't have to go anywhere, lucky devils! Still, I suppose that's another matter! My cousin became a Buddhist for a bit while he was at university and shaved his head, and even the Beatles got into that transcendental stuff, didn't they? So, Paul, how about it? Is there a difference and what made you swap? Oh, and which denomination would you be in if you were alive today?

Yours,

Andy

P.S. By the way, I showed your letter to my RE teacher—he said he hardly supposed it had really come from you and then smiled rather thinly (he's a miserable bloke) and said, 'No doubt it's a 21st-century amanuensis.' I was blowed if I was going to give him the satisfaction of asking him what the hell he was on about. His name is Mr Cork and he loves making people feel small and silly. To be honest, he's been a real turn-off about religion altogether. He pulls it all to pieces, chews it, spits it out in nasty little chewed-up dry balls, and wonders why we don't seem to want to swallow everything he says!

P.P.S. Can I have your signature for a few of my mates? I'm sending this letter via my mum and her church, so I've put some bits of paper in. I promise I won't sell them!

Dear Andy

How amazingly alike you make all the main world religions seem. And there is quite a lot of truth in what you say. They do all have rules and rituals associated with them, and they are all intended to offer an explanation of why we are here and where we are going. But Andy, things haven't changed so very much, you know. There were as many different religions to choose from when I was around as there are in your time. We had our own version of 'Eat, drink, and be happy, because tomorrow may never happen.' It was called Epicureanism and it offered the chance to have a really good time now because being happy was all that really mattered.

Then there was emperor worship. Caesar Augustus was the first emperor to claim personal divinity—a convenient religion for keeping control and demanding loyalty, as your Henry the Eighth discovered so many years later when he chose to become head of the Church in England. Then we had Stoicism, which had all the pantheistic, laid-back fatalism of your hippy religions. I don't think any chose to drop out of society completely, but I remember that 'to live according to nature' was their watchword, and several varieties of cults created the sort of spiritual hunger that drove people like your cousin to search for answers.

As a boy in Tarsus, I, like you, knew boys who had far more freedom to question and choose, but in a way it was easier for me, because there was no question of who I worshipped. You see, while I came across some wonderful ideas from the philosophical writings of many of my Greek and Stoic contemporaries, and often used their ideas in later life to get across points to my Gentile audiences, I was a Jew by race and religion, worshipping the one true God. I saw no need to search for answers. We had them all—or so I thought. You ask me what made me 'swap'. I suggest that you take more than just a glance at what my friend Luke wrote, and you might find out what happened to make me realize that I had not got every answer after all. Andy, when you say I 'swapped' from being a Jew to being a Christian, you haven't quite understood. I'll try to explain.

All Jews believed then (and still believe in your age) that one day the true Messiah would come. He was to be the direct descendant of King David, and when he came he was to restore Israel to its position of glory. Now, as far as I was concerned, there was absolutely no way Jesus could be the longed-for Messiah. A vagrant from peasant stock, with a Galilean accent, hardly seemed the logical candidate. What's more, the fact that, far from restoring the kingdom to Israel, he was actually crucified by the foreign occupying power was, to me, a contradiction in terms. Then there were his followers. I'd see them gathered in Solomon's porch on my way into the temple. To me, steeped in the Torah which I knew to be the very word of God, they seemed disorganized and confused and extremely dangerous. They had nothing written down but seemed to be relying on the things their so-called Christ had said before his death, showing utter contempt not just for the Law but for national customs dating back to the time of Moses. They were actually alleging that this Jesus of theirs had been raised from the dead. What really incensed me was the gullibility of many of the temple priests whom they duped into believing their nonsense. My own relatives, Andronicus and Junias, were taken in. I was even more furious when my own teacher, Gamaliel, advised the Jewish authorities not to persecute the traitors but to wait and see whether or not God honoured their beliefs.

Not for me the relaxation provided by our equivalent of a good game of cricket. Now, how did I put it when I wrote to my church in Galatia? Something like, 'I forged ahead in Judaism beyond many of my own age and race and I was more exceedingly jealous for the traditions of my fathers.' Looking back, I can see that the spiralling violence of my actions against the followers of this new religion was fuelled by a sense of being God's representative here on earth, fighting alone for what was right—for the truth.

It wasn't just a case of giving orders for others to carry out, either. I freely admit that I actually approved of Stephen's death and, as I set out on the night that was to change my life literally for ever, I was blazing with anger, fully intending to drag the Christians in Damascus out of their homes myself and send them in chains back to Jerusalem. How much do you know about that night, Andy? Not too much, I would say, judging by your questions so far!

Well what happened was... No, I'm not going to tell you, you can read about my experience in Luke's account! I have, of course, been aware over the years of how scholars have tried to explain what happened to me in terms ranging from epilepsy to sunstroke, and even temporary insanity brought on by the repression of guilt caused by my involvement with the murder of Stephen and others. Andy, all that matters is that I saw and heard Jesus say to me, 'Why are you persecuting me?' and a dazzling light of understanding flashed on at last in my brain. In that same moment, I fell from my horse and was struck blind. As miracles go, I suppose it could be said to be less dramatic than the parting of the Red Sea or the turning of water into wine, but for me it was as though everything I had searched for, everything I had fought for, fell into place in a quite extraordinary way—the look on Stephen's face when he was about to face a ghastly death, as though he was at peace with God in a way I never had been; the joy and confidence of Peter and his companions, as though they feared nothing.

It wasn't a case of 'swapping'; it was a case of realizing that the truth had been there all the time, but I hadn't understood—the truth that Jesus was not the destroyer of the Law but the fulfilment of it, and that in becoming his follower I was becoming a fulfilled Jew. Israel was not going to be liberated from the colonial yoke of Rome. I was to see the coming of the kingdom in people's lives, not in territories. Do you understand, Andy? Don't worry if you don't. I had enough difficulty explaining it to people in my own time, let alone in yours! What happened after that is history, but those few seconds changed me for ever. From that moment on, I proclaimed Jesus, the risen Messiah, and came to believe that only through belief in him could we inherit the kingdom of God. The Law which I had promoted so zealously as the way to heaven was, in fact, a stumbling-block which could only lead to death. The very suffering of Jesus, his rejection and death, actually *proved* his Messiahship, revealing his glory as never before. As a Pharisee, I had tried to be good enough for heaven, struggling daily to keep every single law of Moses. Under law, we lived in fear of God. Now I saw that the law was not God's last word. I saw that his love was so great for us that he solved the problem of righteousness, sin and forgiveness by allowing his Son to die for us while we were still sinners, and that now, through grace, we could approach him in love and gratitude. Truth remained a passion for me, but now the truth as I saw and believed it was the same as that understood by Peter, John and Stephen.

My dear little brother, please don't allow yourself to be poisoned by the liberality of your day. Don't be afraid to look at every religion, examine every philosophy, face every challenge. But don't leave it there. You say that there are religions where people search for mystery, but the greatest mystery of all is that, through Christ, Christianity offers us a relationship with the living God. Search, Andy. Search, and you will find the extraordinary truth for yourself that Christ himself, the hope of glory, can be in you, and that you can reflect the image and glory of God himself. How? Because the Holy Spirit can implant the very life of Christ in you. Why? Because part of God's glorious plan, thought out when he first created the world, is that you, Andy—like me, despite the fact that we are sinners—have the opportunity to receive the blinding, healing light of his blessing, because of the death of his Son. I suspect that your Mr Cork has not yet received this blessing or he wouldn't be spitting out little dry wads of lifeless knowledge.

Oh, and Andy, an 'amanuensis', just so that you don't have to feel silly again, is a sort of secretary. We were quite a civilized bunch and it was common practice to dictate letters and sign them just as it is in your day. Sometimes the secretaries would put in little bits of their own, like Tertius did at the end of my letter to the Romans, and sometimes I would give them the general gist of what I wanted to say and they would write it out for me to check, and I would add my own greeting at the end. Usually I just poured out everything I wanted to say and left them to tidy the whole thing up, putting in punctuation and polishing the sentences. I bet you wish you had an amanuensis with you in your exams! Of course, the fact that I signed the letters was very important, as my signature would be the only means my churches would have of knowing for sure that the letter was from me, but my writing was rather large and clumsy and I am very, very glad I didn't have to write every letter by hand. However, Andy, because in this case it's what I have said that is vitally important, not the fact that I myself am writing to you, I am not going to send you autographs on bits of paper. I have thrown you the ball of life. Catch it, my dear son, catch it.

Yours,

Paul

Sheila

Dear Paul

I wonder if you could have a word with my husband. I am really worried about him. He works in London and has to put in really long hours, and then top that off with about four hours of train journeys every day. When he gets home I know he could do with relaxing, but he's off down the church just about every evening. He's an elder in our church fellowship, you see. It isn't a full-time job, of course, but you would think it was from the hours he puts in. If it isn't the youth group, it's the prayer meeting or the weekly elders' meeting or the worship committee or visiting. Part of me thinks it's wonderful and part of me resents it a bit, and part of me thinks it's just plain silly. I've asked him to slow down and I've told him I'm worried, but he says he's not going to let people down just because he's a bit tired. Well, last week he had to go to the doctor because he keeps getting indigestion, and the doctor took his blood pressure (routine check-up stuff at our surgery) and reckons it's way up, and that Nick is overloading and in danger of burn-out. So you can see why I'm so worried.

There's something else. I feel a bit disloyal sharing this with you. It's just that he seems to be getting really wound up about everything, which is not like him at all. I know I'm biased, but he's a lovely person, and usually nothing seems to make him angry. But the other day there was something he had to go up to the church for and he found some paint pots that had been left in the kitchen by the Mums and Toddlers group who meet in the hall on Mondays, and he went ballistic. He's nearly fifty and I'm scared stiff that he's going to get ill, Paul. The problem is, if I say something, he will probably quote what you say about 'running the race'. He has always tried to model his ministry on yours and worked so hard to be a good shepherd. Should I try to get him to delegate a few of his responsibilities to someone else? I am so frightened, Paul. Do you think you could possibly find time to write to him?

Yours,

Sheila

P.S. If you think that what he is doing is all right, please don't bother. I know how busy you must be. I live with your greatest fan!

Dear Nick

Greetings to you, dear brother, so beloved of God. Your witness of hard work, your patience and strong faith as an elder of your church have been an example to your fellow followers and a matter for rejoicing.

Your wife, Sheila, tells me that you try to copy the way I worked when I was on earth, and it is true that I encouraged hard work as an ideal to my young churches. I used my tentmaking skills night and day to make the money we needed for sustenance, as an example of the right way to live without being a burden on our fellow men. It is also true that I actually suggested people should copy me, but I added, and this is often forgotten, 'as I copy Christ'.

I, like you, wanted to get it right. Deep down I wanted to be perfect, even though I knew that this wasn't possible, and that it was only through grace that I would be able to enter the gates of heaven. Even though I knew that we are saved only as those escaping through the flames are saved, I wanted to bring something out of the fire, however small, to give to God as evidence of my involvement with the building of his Church here on earth. None of these things is wrong, dear brother, and I commend you for your zeal. But your wife tells me you are becoming ill, and I am concerned that you are losing the sense of blessing and peace which can only come from daily contact with our dear Lord. I cannot insist that you copy me in taking rest, because I realize you have Luke's record of my relentless lifestyle to use as evidence against me! I can remind you, though, of some things that I had to learn along the way which might help you and Sheila to make some decisions about your future.

The role of leadership is, as you know, God-given and Spirit-anointed, however manmade the selection may seem. I also know you appreciate that it is a privilege to be entrusted, despite our obvious unworthiness, to pass on the riches of the gospel, whether through the gift of preaching or service. As an elder, you have clearly felt the same compulsion as myself to build faith where there was doubt and to lay firm foundations of control and communal responsibilty. You have tried to be a facilitator, a teacher, and a servant of your fellowship, and you have tried to do all these things with the right attitude of heart. I know all too well how hard it is sometimes to beseech and urge your fellow Christians when your inclination is to impose your convictions on those you lead, especially when you genuinely want the best for them. I so wanted my converts to feel rooted and established in the love of Christ, to grow towards maturity, 'attaining'—as I put it to my European flock—'to the whole measure of the fullness of Christ'. I wanted them to have all the blessings that I had, to experience his love as I had, and to want more than anything else to live lives worthy of him. I wanted it so much that it hurt. In fact, I think I even compared the pain to that of childbirth on one occasion —maybe, in retrospect, a slight presumption on my part!

Oh yes, my brother, I remember very well the deep exhaustion and occasional heartbreak I experienced as I tried to be a responsible parent to my newborn churches. What I had to learn, Nick, was that however much I wanted all these things for my children in Christ, I couldn't make them happen. These churches didn't belong to me, they belonged to God. I may have been responsible for planting the seed, or in some cases for sharing the watering of the plant, but it was only God who could make the plant grow. It therefore didn't matter whether the work was done by myself or by others. All that mattered was that God was involved. I learned eventually to trust this truth and also to give thanks to God for allowing me to join with my fellow Christians in his triumphal procession as spreaders of the fragrance of the knowledge of himself. My task and responsibility to my flock was to make sure I didn't create a situation where they remained dependent on me—to enable them to grow up to a point where they could recognize their self-sufficiency in the Spirit and discover that Christ was formed in them.

There was a second, more practical reason for this which may or may not apply to you, Nick, depending on what God's plans may be for you in the future. Although I longed to stay and pastor my churches, the Spirit was constantly moving me on (or I was forced to flee for my very life, which may be another more prosaic way of saying the same thing!) Saying goodbye was a way of life. I had therefore to learn how to pastor the pastors, so that when I was forced to leave an area and move on, I could feel it was all right to do so—not easy.

My church in Thessalonica was so very young, and still in need of my pastoring when I had to leave it. I missed them terribly and worried about them constantly—and with reason, for they did indeed suffer at the hands of the Jews. I never did get back to them, although I was able eventually to send Timothy to guide them into maturity.

I remember the frustrating occasion when I felt compelled to leave Troas, even though I thought I was just on the verge of a breakthrough, and that the people were hungry for the gospel.

Then there was my church in Ephesus. Granted, I was allowed to stay with them for a considerable time, but after the silversmiths' riots I had to get out in a hurry, and, do you know, I never did manage to get back. The nearest I got was an emotionally charged meeting with my eldership team when I docked overnight at Miletus on my way to Jerusalem. I had to tell them that I had a rather overwhelming spiritual hunch that I was not going to see them again, and I warned them about the dangers that lay ahead of them—false teachers who would appear like vicious wolves endangering the life of the flock. I gave them over to God's care and we wept together as we hugged and prepared to part for what turned out to be the last time. It hurt far more than the floggings I occasionally had to endure.

The reason I have shared all this with you is that I want to bring to you one thing I said to those dear friends. I urged them to keep a watch over themselves in order that they could be good overseers of the flock. If the shepherds became too tired, too battered and too bruised by their years of service, they would not be sufficiently vigilant and the wolves might creep in. Nick, you are not well. You are exhausted and it would seem that you are suffering from stress. You might be in danger, not only to yourself, but also to the folk you care about so much.

So what I urge you to do is to seek advice. There is no need to feel that you must battle alone. From prison and from overseas I wrote trying to help my churches to see how much they needed to rely on each other's strengths, so that they could stand firm in one spirit and contend as one body for the faith of the gospel. Again and again I urged them to live in peace with one another, to do nothing out of selfish ambition or vain conceit, but to look after each other and, when appropriate, to delegate responsibility. This corporate life would not only curb such excesses but also guard against the problem of individual hero-worship. Oh yes, Nick, this was a problem just as much then as it is for you now. Apollos, or Paul? What rubbish! No wonder I made sure that I didn't baptize more than I absolutely had to. The only gospel is and was the gospel of our Lord Jesus Christ. Praise be.

Nick, may I urge you to give serious consideration to all I have said, and to seek your fellow elders' advice and the Lord's will for your future and that of your church. And may the God of peace sanctify you through and through so you can continue to be part of his glorious army in whatever role might be yours.

Your brother,

Paul

✑ Tricia ✑

Dear Paul

I am in the middle of the very worst week in my entire life. Nothing you can say or do will help me and my family, but I just want to talk to you so much. My darling, darling daughter has died, Paul. She has gone. I still can't take it in, but each morning I wake up feeling sick and strange, and then I remember. She died suddenly, you see. We didn't know she was even ill. She was so lovely, Paul, such a good, good girl. She was clever and kind and always lovely to her little brother. She never went through any nasty patches. Well, not really. We love—loved—her so much. What can you say to me, Paul? Where is she? Why has this happened to us? She didn't deserve to die.

She was 17, just going into the sixth form at school, her future ahead of her. She went to church most Sunday evenings and to youth group. I don't know if she had actually made the decision, if you know what I mean—I don't think she felt there was any urgency. She hasn't always found it easy to go along with everything the church said, but she was full of hope, determined that she and her friends would make a difference. And I know she prayed sometimes, especially for her friends.

How can this have been what God intended for her, Paul? Someone the other day asked me if I felt angry. I just feel devastated and very confused, especially with you! You see, we've had loads of cards and one of them had some of your words in it. They churned me up a bit. It almost sounded as if you thought death was a good thing to happen. I know you can't have meant that, even allowing for the fact that you couldn't know how it feels to have a child die. But for a moment I hated you—hated your complacency, your matter-of-factness.

I don't feel that now. All I want is to know—well, you know what I want to know. Please help. I feel utterly, utterly lost. Can you help me?
Yours,

Tricia Bowland

Dear Tricia

May I first extend my deepest sympathy to you and your family. You are quite correct. There was nothing in my experience to equal your present tragedy.

Tricia, I am not at liberty to tell you what I know you want to hear more than anything in the world. What I can do is to tell you that you must ask for the faith to trust that, just as surely as Eutychus was brought back to life in this world, so will your daughter be in the next. She will stand before Christ's throne, and because of what he did for her two thousand years ago, she will stand holy, faultless and irreproachable. Tricia, I am going to try to explain to you what I meant when I said that 'for me to live is Christ, to die is gain'. I wasn't saying that death is enjoyable. Neither was I being morbid. What I was trying to say was that, in a very real sense, when we accept the Lord Jesus into our lives we experience the only death that really counts—the death of death. From that moment, our lives become hidden in Christ. He is our life and we can never die in any sense that matters. It is just a matter of time before we are allowed to go home, and in the meantime we have to get on with living in our bodies here. We try to make it our goal to please him, but while we are on earth we will never be able to fulfil the longing we experience to actually be with him. I make this sound very matter-of-fact, but it was a passion which burned in me. The more I got to know him, the more I yearned to be with him. After all, all the apostles except me had actually known him while he was here on earth. I lived impatiently with the truth that I simply had to wait until I was allowed to go home to live my life in his presence. So, in other words, while I knew that I had Christ in me in this life, only death would allow me to have what I wanted most in the world, to actually be with him. It was therefore a very personal desire that I expressed when I was writing to my dear friends in Philippi.

Dearest Tricia, it is my deepest wish for you to understand that although it is quite awful for you no longer to have your wonderful daughter, it is not death that has taken her from you. Death has no power over her. When our Lord and Saviour died on the cross, he didn't do so in order to conquer Rome, although, in my ignorance, I had believed that Rome was the enemy our Messiah would deal with. No, indeed, our Lord was after a far more dangerous adversary, namely death itself. At the moment Christ died, death lost its sting completely. The last enemy had been destroyed, swallowed up in victory; and nothing could separate God's children from him ever again.

So Tricia, she has simply gone home before you. Her house was ready before yours. Having served him in her short life, she can now enjoy him for ever more. She can never be hurt. She can never die. But, of course, you cannot fully understand this. Your tears tell the truth. You have lost your most precious jewel and for a time nothing will even begin to explain it to you or enable you to rejoice in her blessings. All I can promise you, my dear friend, is that as long as we are on earth we can only ever expect to catch an occasional glimpse of the truth. I used a very simple illustration all those years ago which I believe will still have the same relevance to you. I said that while we are on earth it is as if we can only see a very poor reflection of something which we know by faith is the truth himself. It is frustratingly hazy and blurred. Only when we have passed through the gate which we still call death, but which we should call life, will we see him face to face and be able to know him as clearly as he knows us.

In the meantime, I know that this same risen Lord, Jesus himself, so aptly described by Isaiah as being 'a man of sorrows and familiar with suffering' will want to be there for you in your agony, and I know he will be willing to receive all you need to say, so talk to him.

Your friend,

Paul

Dear Paul

I am sorry to pester you again so soon, but something has happened which has upset me even more, and I don't know who else to turn to. My son James was picking up the post from our front mat. There was a copy of the church magazine with a special insert saying when the funeral is to be, and some bills, but almost all of it was letters and cards expressing their sympathy and saying something lovely about our beautiful girl. And there was something else. There was a note in an unmarked envelope which simply said 'THE WAGES OF SIN IS DEATH'. I found James all screwed up in an armchair, shouting and screaming in his shock and grief, this horrible bit of paper in his hand. I know there are and have always been sick people around, but it's got inside my head and I can't get it out of my thoughts. Lucy had some rather odd schoolfriends and she had recently taken to wearing those awful clunky shoes and loads of black, and she had even had an eyebrow pierced. She wasn't like some of her friends who used to go out for an evening looking as though they were going trick-or-treating, if you know what that means, with loads of black lipstick and dark smudgy eyes. But she'd had this ink tattoo done on her ankle and she did look a bit different from most of her church friends. Her granny and I used to laugh about it. We knew she hadn't really changed, but I know some of the older folk in the church had problems with the way she looked.

Paul, tell me it can't be true. Tell me this illness which has taken her away isn't her fault. I don't really believe it can be so, or that God could be so cruel or so lacking in insight, but…

I tried to take in what you said in your letter but it was hard, you know. Now this.

Yours,

Tricia

Dear Tricia

I am deeply sorry to hear what has happened to you and to your family. Now, I have two things to say to you and I want you to listen carefully because you are in danger. You are very vulnerable at the moment. It is essential that you keep your eyes firmly on the one who loves you and see to it that no one takes you captive through the hollow and deceptive philosophy which depends on human tradition and the basic principles of this world rather than on Christ.

First, you say that Lucy had a tattoo on her ankle. Did you know she had another stamp on her? Not easily visible, and definitely not removable with soap and water. At the moment she accepted Jesus as her Lord, she received a spiritual birthmark. She was stamped with the seal of the Holy Spirit of the promise who is the pledge of our inheritance. That is what her Father in heaven saw when he looked at her. You say she dressed slightly outrageously. The young have always wanted to make their mark, always wanted to outdo their elders in their passion and their zeal. She was no exception. What made her exceptional was that she seemed to have found a way to be all things to all people without compromising herself. She prayed for her friends. She knew them well enough to realize that they were not yet ready to see what she had as something they needed, and she loved them well enough to realize that prayer was the only way she could hope to ensure their future freedom.

Now, I think that's enough said on that subject, don't you?

Let us now look at the content of the note. First of all, and without trying to justify myself, I want to quote the whole sentence as I wrote it. What I actually said was, 'The wages paid by sin is death; the gift freely given by God is eternal life in Christ Jesus our Lord.' I did not mean that if you die you must have sinned. Why would I have said that? Everyone sins and everyone dies, so it would have been rather a waste of paper, wouldn't it? Don't forget, my letters were written on papyrus, which was costly and complicated to produce. The strips of bulrush pith of which our paper was constituted had to be imported from the banks of the Nile, so I'd hardly waste it on saying silly, obvious things of no worth. No, what I meant was that the evil one is the ultimate deceiver. The wage he has in store for his servants is spiritual death. Try to remember what I said to you in my last letter. For God's children, death is simply the door through which they run into his presence. For the slaves captured during their lifetime by the evil one, death is the door to a life without Christ. You say your daughter was full of hope—hope for the future. You too can have hope, hope in a God who does not lie and who gave his promise before time began that life in Christ is eternal. Wear this hope as your helmet to protect you from the arrows of doubt with which the evil one will try to pierce your thoughts.

Lastly, I want to refer briefly to the writer of the letter. I want you to pray for her because she is in even greater danger than you. I fear that, despite her involvement in your church, she is in fact a servant of sin, feeling no obligation to uprightness and having the desire to dominate and degrade. May your faith depend not on human wisdom, but on the power of God. Always remember, dear Tricia, that God at his most foolish is wiser than the cleverest person, and at his weakest is stronger than human beings at their strongest.

Yours with love and concern for you all,

Paul

~ *Steve* ~

Dear Paul

I am writing to you for advice, spurred on, I have to confess, by my wife, Phil. The thing is, for some time now I have been becoming increasingly disturbed by things that are happening at my place of work.

There is, as you may or may not know, a general acceptance of petty pilfering in most office set-ups nowadays, and I suppose I haven't really felt my faith to be challenged particularly by the pinching of a few paper-clips. But things are happening now which feel a lot more serious and I'm not sure what to do. I've known for some time that most of my colleagues have a tendency to inflate their expenses, but so far I haven't had to make a stand on it personally. Maybe I should have challenged them on it but I haven't, and anyway most of them know I go to church and I suppose I've felt it important that they don't have the chance to put me into a 'religious crank' category.

That's what I've told myself, anyway, but last month we all attended a sales conference, staying in the same hotel and enjoying the same privileges. I enjoy a drink like the next man, and I have to confess that we all had a few good evenings at the company's expense—as far as I was concerned, quite legitimately. There were some nice pubs in the town, and rather than eating in the stuffy, formal and ludicrously over-priced restaurant in the hotel, we used to enjoy our suppers of pie and mushy peas washed down by a few beers. We each kept a tab and paid up at the end of each evening, keeping the bills. Well, the conference finished after lunch on Thursday and when I went to reception to check out, I happened to be standing behind one of my colleagues when he paid his bill. I was extremely puzzled to hear that his bill had come to considerably more than mine, and even more disconcerted when he called me to one side and explained that he had claimed for dinner in the hotel each evening. To my amazement, it came to £85 for the three evenings, instead of the £22 which our pub meals had actually cost. His argument, produced lightly and confidently, was that we could have eaten in the hotel if we had wanted to, and the hotel was used to producing bills like this, so where was the harm? I couldn't think of a good answer but consoled myself that, so long as I didn't lie myself, my conscience was clear, and that what other people decided to do was, after all, up to them, and the whole thing would blow over quietly. I was, of course, wrong.

On Friday morning when I got into work, I was collared in my office by the rest of my conference colleagues who asked me to pretend I had lost my hotel receipt and say that, as it would have been the same as theirs, could I simply claim the same? I told them I didn't think I could do that, and they said didn't I care about landing them in the you-know-what, and how could I call myself a Christian when I put my _____ principles before my mates. They made me feel a pompous prig and I found myself longing to just laugh and go along with it, until I thought of what Phil would have to say!

Anyway, I said I'd think about it and that I'd tell them what I had decided to do by Monday, and when I got home Phil suggested I write to you. She said that everyone at church was buzzing about how you were actually replying to people and what you were saying. I know this is a cheek, but is there any chance of your replying by Monday, do you think? I've worked really hard at trying to be one of them, even though I often feel like a foreigner, so different is the language of their life from mine, and I don't want to blow it now. Neither do I want to let down myself, Phil, and God.

Yours sincerely,

Steve

Dear Steve

First, I do sympathize with your dilemma. Living in the world but not being of the world carries with it a tension in your lifestyle just as much as it did in ours.

I know from personal experience what it feels like to represent something which seems foolish to those around. To many I must have looked like a misguided clown being constantly knocked down— lowered down a wall in a basket on one occasion, mistaken for a god on another and stoned within an inch of death on yet another. 'Is all this really necessary?' is the question I asked myself. 'Surely there must be a slightly less humiliating way to sell the good news?' But the truth is, Steve, there isn't. You see, we are not just peddlers of the truth, a day job which can be temporarily suspended when we want to relax. We are it—the good news, I mean. We are a living advertise-ment. That means, to change analogies from shop floor to army, we are always on duty, and even when we cannot be seen by other people we can be seen by God, our commander-in-chief. A soldier's training has always been gruelling and involved a lot of struggling through mud in order to increase physical and mental stamina, and the training for a soldier of Christ is equally tough for those who seriously want to join his army. So the situation you are in is not just a petty problem confined to your workplace, but crucial to your standing as a soldier of Christ, and it needs addressing seriously, as I think you realize. In writing to me, I suspect you know my answer could be tough.

Let me reiterate my sympathy. I gather you really like some of your work colleagues and, deep in your heart, I suspect you envy their freedom. That is natural. We were never asked to judge others; we can safely leave that to a far wiser magistrate than us. We are asked to love our neighbours as Christ himself did, to have a heart for the lost as he did. One thing to bear in mind is that, at the point when a sheep is getting lost, he is not aware of the danger he is in and therefore doesn't cry out in need. Your friends are clearly blissfully ignorant of the peril they are in as they stray further and further away from what that built-in 'shepherd', their conscience, says to them.

You, with the benefit of having the Holy Spirit to guide you, need to care sufficiently deeply for their souls to want to work out the best strategic plan to save them before it is too late. It won't be easy, because they won't want to be rescued: they are having too much fun. Also, they see you as a threat to their future security as far as their money and jobs are concerned, and this will make them angry.

I had a few experiences of this during my ministry, of course. In Ephesus, my talk of the one true God did little to endear me to the silversmiths, who made a nice living beating out effegies of the goddess Diana, but the nearest I came to your experience was probably when I first arrived in Philippi. There was a pathetic slave-child there who was being horribly exploited by her owners. Luke was with me at the time, and you may remember from his account of it that she was possessed by a demon who allowed her to see into the future. This demon recognized the Holy Spirit in us and persisted in making this poor child follow us, shouting out who we were. Well, as living advertisements for God go, this was not the most effective, as you can imagine, and after a few days I could stand it no longer. Her healing was essential for her own sanity and also for mine! Being the sole representative (pun intended) of my Lord, it fell to me, in the name of Jesus, to command the spirit to come out of her. Well, as you can imagine, this went down very badly with her owners, who saw their livelihood disappearing before their very eyes. Their anger proved very uncomfortable for me, but then, there is and always has been a cost and at least I didn't have to buy her freedom with my life. But I'll come back to that later.

The other reason it won't be easy is because of you. Steve, I want to ask you one or two questions. First, are you genuinely concerned about what to do for the benefit of your friends or are you afraid for yourself? I was often afraid. But I did have a confidence that I suspect you have not yet got, that what I said and did was a message from God to those I encountered and that my personal safety here was of little importance compared to my safety in eternity. So the next question I ask you, Steve, is this. Do you have the confidence in Christ to open your ears and your heart to him over this weekend and on Monday so that what he needs to say to your work colleagues can be said through you? It's not going to be an easy few days, because there will be another speaking to you this weekend—the one who desperately tries to keep God's children from meeting him; the one whom, because our sinful natures are not totally transfigured when we are reborn as children of God, we tend to listen to. You see, up to that point we are literally slaves, with sin as our owner, just as surely as it owned the girl in Philippi. Now, even though we want to do our Father's will and do what is right, we can't. Instead, we do what we hate even when we know it's wrong. We can't help it because sin is stronger than we can ever be in our own strength. So, if in our hearts we really want to be God's willing servants instead of sin's slaves, then we have to look elsewhere than our own virtuous natures to set us free from our former lifestyle. We have to look at Jesus and remember that he has already freed us from slavery to our old master. We need to breathe in the power of his life-giving Spirit, who will enable us to resist the devil with confidence and to start behaving like the free people we are. Salvation from sin is a present reality which begins at our conversion but continues to be worked out throughout our lives. It gives us the potential to know in practice what it feels like to resist what is wrong and to do what is right.

You are now a representative of God. You are his son. When people meet you, they come as near to meeting him as they ever will. Let's look at some of the features of your old nature, which currently share the Holy Spirit's rightful position as commander-in-chief in your everyday decisions, and give such a poor impression of your Saviour.

You say you do not want to appear a religious crank, and as I said before, I understand, but what do they see when they see you, Steve? I know you are not involved with sexual sin and I know you don't swear or bully. However, you do want and need to be liked and accepted. You don't like causing ripples. You need to feel secure, and therefore you are afraid of losing your chance of promotion. Although you despise these qualities, they are an integral part of you. On the sin scale they may not seem too gross, but Jesus himself linked cares of the world with debauchery as equal examples of the things which keep human beings from God. Money is and always has been a great danger to people. It is so often revered and even worshipped, and that makes God angry and sad. He is asking you to work out your salvation with fear and trembling, dependent only on him. Because I fear for you, let me just remind you of why we need to try to stand against sin—why what you do on Monday matters so much.

I have to tell you, Steve, that God does not like sin. The fact that he is willing to forgive our sins again and again does not mean that he condones them. The reason Jesus had to die was that God could not solve the sin problem in any other way while still remaining holy. You see, the Law was impossible to keep (I should know—as a Pharisee I tried hard enough and ended up full of anger and hatred). Because it was impossible, this meant we could never be good enough to earn our way into heaven and that the evil one owned us. Sin could rightfully claim ownership of us for eternity because of proof in the form of a list, as long as your arm, of times when we had failed to keep God's Law. We were utterly helpless to save ourselves from the death penalty we deserved. So what did this God, who represents everything good and holy and pure, do? He loved us so much that he took on the collective sins of the whole world and died for all of us. In other words, by taking the list of our sins and nailing it to the cross, he bought our freedom in the only possible way.

My dear young teachers so often had to stand against the temptations that their sinful world offered, and again and again I had to remind them why they needed to stand firm, just as I am reminding you. I was always going on about it, but perhaps most succinctly to Titus. I said to him what I want now to say to you. 'When the kindness and love of God our Saviour for humanity was revealed it was not because of any upright actions we had done ourselves; it was for no reason except his own faithful love that he saved us, by means of the cleansing water of rebirth and renewal in the Holy Spirit which he has so generously poured over us through Jesus Christ our Saviour; so that justified by his grace we should become heirs in hope of eternal life.' This, I promised Titus, is doctrine you can rely on. I think I put it rather well, though I say it myself!

I also had to remind them *how* to do it. Steve, one of the most pernicious ways in which your God-given supplies get sabotaged is by the things that Jesus said, and the things I said, being taken out of context and garnished prettily, when in fact they were intended as hard rations for soldiers in the field. And that's just where you are, right now, whether you want to be or not. It is very demoralizing to go into battle on an empty stomach, so let us feed on some of God's wonderful truths, and see if maybe they will be sufficient to sustain you over this weekend's preparations and through Monday's fight.

First of all, there is something I said to the Roman church. Bear in mind how vulnerable this small band of soldiers must have felt, surrounded as they were by visual displays of human wealth and power in the epicentre of civilization. I reminded them that what, on the surface, might look impressive was in fact nonsense, and that in claiming to be wise without God these apparent conquerors had become utter fools instead. Neither were the enemy to be let off or considered blameless in their ignorance, because since the very beginning of time, God has set before them such a visual display of splendour in the form and wonder of the universe that instinctively they have known of his existence but have deliberately refused to acknowledge him. Similarly with us: we are under no obligation whatsoever to follow our old sinful nature, however persuasive it may be. We are not slaves any more. We are God's very own children. We can call out to him, 'Daddy, Daddy, help us', and he surely will, although what form that will take I cannot tell you.

So, Steve, however alone and feeble you may feel on Monday, remember to keep your eyes fixed on the one who can help you— your very own Father God. Nothing can separate us from his love. Death can't and life can't. Goodness me, even the powers of hell itself can't. There may be a cost in standing against what you believe in your heart is wrong, but whatever your fears and worries, nothing can separate you from your Father. There is more. It just might be that God has appointed you as his special ambassador to your friends at work. If this is so, then the Holy Spirit has already been at work in their hearts and all he needs is for you to be a living sacrifice. Be prepared to fight, prepared to lay down your future security, in order for him to break the bond which binds these men to their present owner and bring them safely home.

A soldier is never sent empty-handed into battle. God will let you wear his armour into battle. Put on his breastplate of righteousness and wear the helmet of salvation. You can carry faith as your shield to defend you against your opponent—and I don't mean the disapproval of your work colleagues, I mean the arrows of the evil one. Beware of him. He is no gentleman prepared to challenge you with pistols at dawn. He will fight dirty to keep his slaves from hearing the truth. But, dear Steve, remember this for me. You do not have to win them over by your cleverness or your wit. You do not have to pick up worldly weapons of subterfuge, cowardice, aggression and spite. In fact, it is imperative that you lay such things down before you go to work on Monday. You carry in your possession the good news of peace, truth that can set them free; and the sword you are allowed to carry, in the form of God's word, is the only one sharp enough to cut the bonds of the evil one.

Just one last thing. Tell Phil to pray for you all the time. You need protection constantly at the moment and you need the Holy Spirit to keep you vulnerable and alert so that you will be able to hear what he is telling you to do and say.

May God lead you safely out into battle, dear children.

Paul

⁓ *Deborah and Sandy* ⁓

Dear Sir

It is against my better judgment that I forward the accompanying letter from my young client Sandra Jones. In replying, may I ask you to show sensitivity to the high level of rejection Sandra has already experienced in her fifteen years.

She tells me that she hasn't mentioned in detail the severity of the physical abuse she and her sister suffered at the hands of her psychotic mother. Neither does she apparently mention just how many foster placements have broken down through her inability to control destructive behaviour. I don't know if you are aware of a sad scenario we are all too familiar with in our work. There is a sub-conscious need in a rejected child to test the tolerance limit of the foster parents in an attempt to understand why her own parents didn't want her. This testing can show in disruptive, aggressive and extremely antisocial behaviour. Naturally there is major input from social services but it is often insufficiently effective and when place-ment collapses, sabotaged irreparably, it is further proof to the child that he/she is unlovable.

Sandra was born as the result of one of several affairs which had taken place shortly after her mother's marriage. Neither the husband nor Sandra's father remained on the scene and, since her mother's imprisonment for extreme physical abuse of both girls, Sandy has had no contact with family members. Sandra's period in the latest resid-ential unit has been reasonably successful. However, her need to belong to a real family resulted in her being highly susceptible to the ridiculous offer, by visiting preachers at her school assembly, of instant acceptance into a church 'family'. Just a short walk to the front, a quick kneel down and she was 'in'. No ghastly primary interviews to ascertain possible compatibility, no vetting of the family, no contracts drawn up between my client and her prospective carers. Sandy claims she experienced extraordinary feelings of joy at the moment she was

111

prayed for. I wonder why I am not more impressed, bearing in mind the highly charged atmosphere and her pathetic desire to fulfil her deepest needs! She has since—surprise, surprise—been made to re-experience many all-too-familiar feelings of uselessness!

I am extremely angry and ask you, please, to prevent further damage by advising her to quit her part in this charade as soon as possible.

Yours sincerely,

Deborah Owen (Ms)

Dear Mr Otarsus

My social worker said she would see you get this. I don't write letters much so I hope you can read it. I want to ask you something. My mum hit us about when we was kids and got done. The social took Donna and me, we wasn't good with our foster parents and they turned round and said they didn't want us no more so we went in this unit. It was all right. Donna got into trouble and had to go in the secure but I was all right. I was never no good at school but I was all right in the unit. Anyway, at school they had this special thingy and a band came. They was well good. Better than we was expecting. They told us God loves us and wants us in his family and that what we done in the past don't matter because you can say sorry, and my mate Julie and me went up. This girl what had been singing told us about her church and it sounded good and she said she'd pick me up from the unit and we went. Everyone was nice and we was told we were part of their family now. They told us about the club what meets on Fridays up their church hall and I went. Julie went as well. I kept going but some of the kids was out of order and told Keith that I was smoking. He turns round and says to me like, You've got to stop smoking. The thing is I was really trying and I really wanted to go but they are stuck-up bastards and I told them, and Mary tell me off for swearing.

Thing is as well, Mary, that's the girl what took us to church, asked Julie round her house and they went to see *Titanic* but they didn't get me to go. I could of gone. I ask Steve what was on duty and he said I could go but they didn't come for me. I was well pissed off and I broke a snooker cue and went in secure for the night. On Sunday the bloke up the front says if you are sad to go and talk with the elders after church and I did and they turn round and say like, You've got to try to stop smoking cos your body is a temple of the holy spirit. I asked them what the f that was and they got really cross and Jenny the other leader says she thinks I need to have prayers to get rid of things, but she doesn't say Julie must and I don't want to. So I turns round and says Stuff you and kicked their pigging little table with the magazines and they say I can't go no more. My social worker says they are well out of order.

Julie is still nice to me at school and she's going camping with them and she says she's going to ask if I can go if I say sorry and promise not to smoke. She says she thinks they will say yes cos they told her they want me back when I am ready to go. She told me about writing to you. She says the elders said that the club could write to you and you'd write back. I'm not in the club till they say but I still want to ask you what you think. Am I still in this family? And another thing. If Jesus loves everybody why will he not love me just because I flipping well smoke?

Love from

Sandy

Dear Ms Owen

May I thank you for the gracious decision you made in allowing Sandy to write to me.

You made clear your misgivings and I appreciate your desire to protect your young client from further hurt. I also acknowledge the reasons for your anxiety. Jesus—as you know, the founder of the Christian Church—set a formidable precedent in the radical way he dealt with those who had been misused by society and those who had deepened their wounds by their self-destructive tendencies. Mary Magdalene is, I understand, perhaps the best-known of those he affirmed into health. The early Church at the time when I was employed tried to be equally committed to creating a structure of care for its weaker members. You may not know this, but there was a structure of social care which successfully eradicated unnecessary financial suffering for those unable to fend for themselves, such as widows and the elderly. Care in the church community was not a bad financial joke created by a government committed only to showing financial savings on paper. I believe you call the abomination of closing centres of care for the most inadequate 'decanting'. Can this really be so? I personally valued highly my social workers—we called them deacons—and you only have to look at the letter I wrote to the very first church I established in Europe to see the value I placed on their role. I say all this to emphasize the value I place on your practical role of support in Sandy's life.

My prayer for my early churches was that their love for each other would get stronger and that they would always show tenderness and compassion and not look after their own interests but also the interests of others. As I have tried to explain to Sandy, the Church under the control of Jesus Christ should function like a healthy body with every bit of it having a role in keeping it that way. All the different parts of the body are supposed to fit together, the whole body being held together by every joint with which it is provided. That's how it is supposed to work, and I have tried to explain it as clearly as possible both to my church in Corinth and also to Sandy. All that said, things went wrong in the churches then and they do now, and it didn't stop me having to spend half my time warning my fragile new churches to hang on to what I'd told them about how Jesus wanted them to live and the other half telling them off for getting it wrong!

So please, Ms Owen, Sandy and I need you to monitor events in the church family that she has joined. I would be most grateful if you would forward me a progress report in due course so that the situation can be reviewed and, if necessary, action taken.

Your fellow worker,

Paul

Dear Sandy

Thank you very much for your most interesting letter which raises some extremely important points. The first is the problem of presenting the gospel, in other words how to tell people about Jesus. When I was working on earth my job was rather like that of your visiting band, only instead of going into schools to speak to teenagers who hadn't heard about Jesus, I went into countries where no one had heard of him! Everywhere I went two thousand years ago there were brave people like you and Julie who were prepared to stand out from the crowd and cross sides from what they believed before to belief in Jesus. It took guts then, and it takes guts now, and one day you'll find out what Jesus himself said about that little walk you and Julie did.

Meeting Jesus feels extraordinary, doesn't it? As though something new is bursting from inside you. I remember the moment when I met Jesus very well, but then it was rather dramatic, involving falling from my horse and being struck blind for a few days! Thankfully it doesn't sound as though your experience was quite as traumatic. But what we do have in common is the discovery that all our problems haven't gone away. In fact, some of mine only began after that meeting. Most of our problems are to do with the fact that, although we have a new life inside us, God doesn't bring about a total transformation in our personalities. In other words, we go on being the same old us! I still had a temper and an impatience with people who couldn't or wouldn't get on with what, to me, seemed the only really important thing to do—telling the world about Jesus. It made me intolerant of others' weaknesses and it was only really when I was in prison in Rome later in my life that I acknowledged my own frailties and need for companionship. You still smoke and swear and try to solve your problems by kicking out. You say you are trying to change, but it's hard. Of course it is, Sandy. That's why Jesus had to die for us. Let me try to explain.

In heaven, where I am now, we live in the most wonderful family, where everyone is perfect in every way, and where God himself is our Father. It is everything you have ever dreamed a foster family could possibly be and a whole lot more, Sandy. But to get here you have to be perfect, which of course you can't be, any more than I could when I lived on earth. Because we can't become all clean and nice and good enough on our own, Jesus came and said he would take all the wrong things we have done and actually die for us. He did this so that even though we are a useless bunch we can go to heaven to live in his family with him when we die. What he didn't say was, 'Everyone who decides to follow me will be perfect and good and nice and clean right now.' So I stayed being me with all my faults while I was on earth and you are staying being you. I tried really hard to be good, and I know you will try really hard to be good and that God will help you to be the best person you can be. But what I had to learn to do was to trust that God loved me so much that absolutely nothing I did could mean he would throw me out of his family as long as I wanted to have him as my Father. And that's what you have to learn too.

Now, the problem is that, just as I stayed being me with all my faults, and you are still you, so, unfortunately, the people who are in your church are still just themselves too! The only perfect family is the one in heaven. Some of your new church family were self-righteous prigs before they met Jesus, and they still are. Some of them can only see the surface of a person and some are afraid of the unfamiliar. They are often kind people and want to do the right thing, but their fear means that they will try to stay safe, and that means not getting too near to things or people that are different. I think Jenny may be one of those. Julie clearly comes from a family where people don't smoke and swear and Jenny feels more comfortable with her than with you. Now, make no mistake, Jesus will want to deal with that fear and will also be wanting to make Julie into the best person she can be, so I think that both of them will find that they need and want to change. But their problems don't show as obviously as yours. What I'm saying, Sandy, is that you may have to be the grown-up for a while and try to understand and forgive your new brothers and sisters. They need you to stay stuck in because you are now a part of their body— I'd better explain that. I hope you can understand what I'm going to say. I tried to explain this to one of my new churches in Corinth but I don't think all of them really understood

Right, here goes.

You know Jesus came and lived on earth. Well, he was a man with a perfectly normal body—although I can't tell you exactly what he looked like. I never actually met him in the flesh, but that's another story! When Jesus was on earth, the whole glorious, loving power of God was held in his one ordinary body. Jesus himself said that when you met him you were actually meeting God the Father.

When that body finally went to heaven on what we call 'Ascension Day', the idea was that the Christians left behind, and all the people who became Christians after that, would join together to become his body on earth. And that includes you. In other words, because you walked up to the front of your school assembly, with all your mates giggling at you, and knelt in front of them and asked Jesus to come into your life, something extraordinary happened. *You* became a part of Jesus' Church, a part of what we call 'the body of Christ'.

So now, everybody who is a Christian is part of Jesus' Church, and when we are all joined together we will show the world a glimpse of Jesus himself. The interesting question is, which bit of the body are you? Whatever that part might be, it is vital to the well-being and beauty of the whole body that you are there. Before you joined the Church, it was missing that bit. As I said to the folk who went to Corinth church, it's silly for an ear to say, 'Because I'm not an eye I don't belong to the body'. I think my words were, 'If the whole body were an eye, where would the sense of smell be?' So, you see, you are as important as anyone in the church, even the elders, and just as special to God, and they are lucky to be just as special as you!

Now I'm going to give you a short lesson in biology. Don't groan, Sandy! What do you call the bony cage that covers your heart and lungs and things? I'm sure I heard you say 'the ribcage'! Well, why did God design you like that? Of course, it's to keep the heart and lungs safe, isn't it? Because without them we could not stay alive. Then there are other vital bits of our bodies, which we don't talk about much, but are just as important to our staying alive, as they clear our bodies of poison and waste. If all our vital organs which keep us alive were all dangling around on the outside they would make the body look horrible and they would get damaged, so God makes sure they are tucked snugly inside walls of muscle, bone and skin.

Sandy, because you are a very new Christian and especially

because you were very hurt when you were a little girl, you are a very special bit of the body that needs to be kept very safe and snug for a while. In that case, I hear you say, why are you being made to feel as if you are left clinging on to the outside?

Now, I don't know if you are going to understand this. Because of the swearing and occasional aggressive behaviour that you have told me about, you probably seem rather a prickly ball to have inside any body! Ouch! What they don't know yet, and what only you and God know, is that the prickles are there to stop you getting hurt any more, and that once you feel warmed up with love you will be able to uncurl and show them a bit more of the real, likable you. Your foster parents got lots of stabs from those old prickles, didn't they? Now, what I am going to ask you to try to do is not going to be easy, but remember, unless they get to find out which bit of their body you are, it might never reflect the beauty of Jesus. So what I want you to do, my little hedgehog, is to let them see the pink of your nose. They will feel safer and more able to hold you closer and actually look at you. I think they will like what they find, but we'll have to see.

Now, about the other thing you said in your letter, the bit about your body being the temple of the Holy Spirit. Yes, I did say it, and yes, I will try to explain why I did. People used to go to the temple to worship God and of course you still do, only now you call them churches. Well, before Jesus came, people believed that God actually lived in the temple. Before Jesus died and went back to being king of heaven, he gave us an introduction to the next part of the mystery we call God.

Jesus said that when we meet him, we meet God our heavenly Father. He went on to tell us about the Holy Spirit who comes to meet us when we say we want to follow Jesus, and, if we ask him to, will come and live inside us. So now we are like little temples with God the Holy Spirit living in us. But, because he comes to live inside us before we have become more like Jesus, our temples can be a bit mucky. Some people's temples are so full of lies and pride and unkindnesses that there is hardly any room. Fortunately, the Holy Spirit will help them have a big spring clean—to say 'sorry' and clear out their rubbish bit by bit. For some people, and especially those who are very successful and rich, it can take ages. I think there might be quite a lot of room in yours already, Sandy, but it's so smoky in there, it's difficult to tell. Clinging on to your need for cigarettes with both hands doesn't make it any easier to grasp the outstretched hand of the Holy Spirit and learn that you can trust him with your very life. Try to read and think about Jesus and concentrate on letting the rest of the body see how unprickly you really are, and you may find it easier than you think to prise one or two fingers away from those cigarettes.

I believe that people are going to see the light of Jesus shining out of your temple one day, my dear child. May his love and the power of the Holy Spirit help you in your uncurling.

Your friend,

Paul

Dear Paul

Does you signing yourself Paul mean you're my friend? Or are you going to smile at me at first and be all nice and then get well angry with me when you know me? See thing is Paul, I tried all that stuff about letting them see me more and it's all gone wrong. I told Jenny about my poems what I wrote when I was in my foster home when I was little and she said she'd like to see them and she was lovely and she cried and said they made her feel well sad and she ask me, like, if she can show the elders cos she said they was really good, and I fort about what you said and said yes and she did. Then one of them elders tells me he thinks that they have got things in them which are not of my new life and I got to burn them because they are part of the old me. What's more he say that you said it Paul. He says you said just forget what is behind. Anyway I went and let them and they told the church how brave I'd been and I let them burn them and then they all hugged me and it was nice and I thought it would be all right but I keep opening my drawers where they always was and I keep crying. I know it sounds silly but I feel like I've killed a bit of me and I feel all sad and bad and lonely. I don't want to be a new me. I want to have my poems. My social worker flipped when I told her and she got well mad with you and with the church and she took me to the doctor and I could see he was angry too.

Thing is Paul, I still want to be in that church family. Sometimes when we're singing I cry but it's different and nice. I still want them to like me but they still don't and they didn't like my poems. Silly thing is I thought they was good. I thought they was the best thing what I've done. And another thing. They was all about my mum and they was writ soon after I wasn't allowed to see her no more and now I can't get into my head with her no more. See, I don't hate her. Well I do sometimes and I want to kill her cos I don't think a mother should hurt her kids ever but I still want her to love me and be my mum. I used to think that she'd turn up one day and say she's sorry like and that she wants us to be together. She's my mum not theirs and what do they know about her and me? They tell me you say to put it all behind me and press on. What's that then Paul? How can I put what's in me out of me? Won't leave much! See I am it—that's what I am. The hittings and the shovings and the dark and the sorries and cuddles and her smell and beery old kisses and cryings. If I take all that out what are they going to see, like you say they should see me? I am me and if they don't like the old me they can stuff it and another thing Paul. Stuff showing them my nose, I'd rather show them the other end at the moment.

Love,

Sandy

Dear Paul

Thank you for your reply, which I found surprisingly sane and supportive. You asked me to report to you on the progress Sandra is making in the church. I am sad to report that the 'placement' is breaking down rapidly! They seem incapable of accepting her as she is, and I am deeply disturbed by their amateur attempts to bring about an immediate change in her personality. I don't think I told you, but among a somewhat motley collection of bits from her past was an exercise book which contains four pages of seven-year-old maths and about 25 poems written by Sandy between the ages of eight and eleven. She first told me of their existence shortly after she became part of my caseload when she was twelve but it took many months before she trusted me sufficiently to show me what she had written. I responded on several levels. A sad relief that here was the proof that dispelled any doubts I might have had about the need for her to be taken into care. A deep sadness that any little child should suffer abuse in such a way. A realization that Sandy, despite her undeveloped communication skills, was an extremely intelligent and sensitive youngster. I responded at the time as honestly as I could and affirmed in her that these poems were a treasure to be kept safely for as long as she needed them—that one day she may be able to separate their content from her consciousness and be able to look at them more clinically, but until then... I felt it wrong to remove them from her in order to photocopy them or to commit to her file any part of the contents of that private little book, a decision I now deeply regret.

I understand she has told you about how she has fallen victim to the amateur blunderings of your so-called 'safe' body. How can you have condoned such simplistic and arrogant interference with a disturbed adolescent? I can no longer justify my silent support of her remaining under the influence of such people. I'd be very interested to know what you can possibly say in their defence.

Yours sincerely,

Deborah Owen

Dear Deborah

Thank you for keeping me informed as to the progress of our young friend. I am deeply disturbed to receive your news.

As I intimated in my first letter, there have always been problems in the Church, although there has in my opinion never been a social system that has offered ordinary people the hope and dignity that Jesus did. He believed in their potential to change and they believed him. Why else would Matthew have left his desk and the security of his tax inspector's job to follow as he did? He must have recognized in the eyes of Jesus a belief that change was possible—that he could become the person he wanted to be. But Jesus never bullied. He never imposed his way on his followers. If Sandy is being bullied into changing on the outside in order to appear to fit the norm, then this may in fact be erroneous teaching. I am not trying to make excuses or to minimize the problems. Jesus told his very first disciples to be on their guard against false prophets who would come to them looking like sheep but in fact be like wild wolves. I had to repeatedly reiterate his concerns. There was the occasion when I realized I was unlikely ever to get back to pastoring my church in Ephesus and that this new church would be very vulnerable. I called an emergency meeting of the elders at Miletus and begged them to make sure they were good shepherds of their flock and to be constantly on the lookout for these wolves. I even warned them that the time would come when some of the men in their church family would tell lies in order to lead believers away from the truth.

So, what, you might ask, is the false teaching in this case?

Well, I don't actually recollect the burning of anything from anyone's past in either Jesus' teaching or my own. However, faith is an amorphous thing and there is sometimes a need to consciously leave behind that which is preventing someone from trusting their safety to the Lord. The essential thing is that what this might be, and the ideal point at which it should happen, varies from person to person. For a certain rich young man, it was his money, but in Matthew's case it was only the money he had cheated out of his customers that he felt compelled to give away. Jesus always had a unique plan for each person who came to him.

From the beginning, we church leaders tried to follow him, as I am sure the leaders in Sandy's church do. Unfortunately, every now and then, leaders get off-track. They stop acting in line with the gospel and start coming up with hard and fast rules which don't in any way reflect the imaginative way Jesus dealt with situations. As you may know, one of my biggest problems was convincing the Jews that the new Gentile converts did not need to be circumcised in order to join the Church. Even Peter, when he visited my home church in Antioch, fell into the trap of feeling the need to impose Jewish customs on the new Christians. I really had to take him to task about it. I had to have a go at the Gentiles as well, as they found it hard to believe that they didn't have to submit to Jewish law in order to be accepted. They just couldn't accept that they didn't have to bring about change in themselves by doing something. I told them, and I would dearly love to tell the elders in Sandy's church, that no one ever received the Holy Spirit because of what they accomplished, and no one ever brought about a miracle because of obeying manmade rules.

It is wrong teaching. Back to the wolves in sheep's clothing. Do you know, even my emergency meeting with the elders in Miletus didn't stop me having to hammer out the same message whenever I wrote to them! The message that we are all as important as each other, that we should always be humble and gentle and tolerant. We should all be at one in what we believe so that we don't get blown about by every shifting wind of teaching by deceitful men. In the very same letter—and I remember being choked with tears as I wrote it— I begged them to be aware of those who lived as enemies of the cross of Christ. Hard as their lives may have been, and mine was not exactly a bed of roses at the time, I wanted them to know that they could be completely at peace with themselves because God loved them so much. If the elders of the church where Sandy is attending at present are expecting more of her than God is, they are getting the message of the gospel badly wrong, however well-intentioned they may be.

Going back to the shepherd image, all baa-ing may sound the same to an outsider, but every mother ewe knows her own lamb and every lamb its mother. Shepherds are supposed to be at least as intelligent as their sheep. If Sandy's elders continue to pursue the idea that she must instigate change in herself, then this may not be the most suitable church for her. She may need more sensitive shepherds who will get to know her and listen to her before deciding before God what she should do.

For now, until I am sure she is in safe hands, will you be her foster shepherd? Even as I ask you, I want to beg you to think very carefully about your response to what has happened to Sandy. I don't mean the most recent amateur bungling, I mean the whole thing. I mean her conversion to Christianity altogether. Be honest with yourself. Is your response motivated by fear of the unknown which the unskilled handling of Sandy comfortably reinforces? I know you will disagree at the moment, but I truly believe, despite recent events, that there is no greener and healthier grass than that belonging to God. Somewhere there is a pasture where she will be able to graze and grow safely.

Yours,

Paul

Dearest Sandy

Thank you for another challenging letter. You are such an interesting letter writer, and I am very sad to hear how unhappy you are. Let me tackle the first bit, where you talked about me saying about leaving everything behind. I've thought long and hard about this and I think the thing that your elders are referring to is something I wrote to my church friends in Philippi. I was in prison in Rome at the time and finding life really hard. I so longed to be able to go and see my friends again and I was anxious that they should keep trying to be as good and as loving to each other as they had been at the beginning. I was trying to help them to see that I really didn't mind putting up with hardships because it was all part of knowing Jesus, and that I even felt closer to him when things were hard because I felt I understood a little more of what he had suffered for us when he allowed himself to be put up on that terrible cross. Somehow I knew that none of what happened to us here on earth would matter once we were with him. So it was about me that I was talking when I said I was trying to press on towards what was ahead and not look back. It wasn't about you.

But I'll tell you something interesting, Sandy. Just after I wrote that, I said something else. I said something like, 'Only let us live up to what we have already attained.' Now, what that means is that God knows exactly what has happened to you. He knows all the things you are frightened about. He knows all about the prickles. He knows how you feel about your mum. He knows why you need to smoke and why you get all hot inside your head and want to kick things. He has seen all your poems. God your Father will never bully you, Sandy. He will never make you do anything you are not ready to do. He will never make you give up anything you are not ready to give up. One day you may be able to ask him to help you to give up smoking, Sandy, but I want to tell you something very important.

Are you ready? Here it is.

You don't have to be afraid any more because nothing, absolutely nothing at all, can separate you from the love of God. He will never let you down, and he will never leave you, whether you manage to give up smoking or not, whether you swear or whether you don't. You are his little girl now and for ever and ever.

All he asks is that you carry on believing in him, and that you talk to him about your hopes and your fears, and thank him for any good things you think of—like how nice it is that Julie still wants to be your friend and that you have a social worker like Deborah who cares about you so much. Jesus never said that life would be easy and my life certainly wasn't! I got shipwrecked and beaten and put in prison! But in the middle of it I knew I was safe. I had a peace which was bigger than anything I could understand. You see, I knew that whatever happened to me, nothing could hurt the important bits, my feelings and my thoughts, because they were safely tucked up in the love of Jesus. Sandy, I'm so sorry about your poems, but do you know what, I think they are still safe in the most important place deep inside your memory. Nothing can take away your memories and your love and need of your mum. One day your friend the Holy Spirit will be able to help you to forgive her and to understand why she did what she did.

Oh, and by the way, are you talking to your new heavenly Father about Deborah? I think God may have a very important job for you to do, my little hedgehog.

May God bless you and keep you safe until we are able to meet one day.

Your big brother,

Paul

✒ Final contact ✒

Good afternoon. This is the reception hall of heaven. I'm afraid there is no one available to take your call at present. If you would like to leave a message after the long harp-tone, we will be glad to consider your request and get back to you as soon as possible.

Just to say—thank you, Paul...

Bibliography

My thanks go to all the authors of the following books who have provided the soundly researched background material to this book.

Going Places with Paul, Donald Fleming, Donors Inc., Australia

Meet Paul, Donald Coggan and David Hope, Triangle, 1997

In the Steps of Timothy, Lance Pierson, IVP, 1995

Reflecting the Glory, Tom Wright, BRF, 1997

Women in the Bible, Mary Evans, Paternoster, 1998

What Saint Paul Really Said, Tom Wright, Lion, 1998

London Bible College evening class lectures on Paul, Peggy Knight